Jeremiah opened his eyes and saw Shelley staring at him.

Shortly after their gazes met, she lowered her head.

He reached out and tucked his finger beneath her chin. "Shelley, I want to be there for you—now and after we find William. Will you at least give me a chance?"

She opened her mouth but quickly closed it. A few seconds later she said, "I don't know, Jeremiah. Everything is so confusing right now. All I can think about is finding my little brother."

Yes, of course. What had Jeremiah been thinking? He wanted to kick himself in the backside for being selfish enough to turn things around to his feelings for Shelley.

"I'm sorry, Shelley. My timing was off. I just want you to know how much I care and that I have confidence we'll find William."

"What if we don't this time?" she asked, fear evident in her expression.

"We will." He took her hand and squeezed it. "We always do."

Debby Mayne is the author of more than sixty novels and novellas. She writes family and faith-based romances, cozy mysteries, and women's fiction. She has also written more than one thousand short stories and articles as well as dozens of devotions for busy women. She has worked as managing editor of a national health publication, product information writer for a TV retailer, a creative writing instructor, and copy editor and proofreader for several book publishers. Debby runs a Southern lifestyle blog, *Southern Home Express*, where she shares cooking tips, recipes and Southern expressions. She and her husband live in North Carolina.

TRUSTING
HER HEART

Debby Mayne

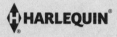

ISBN-13: 978-1-335-46306-7

Trusting Her Heart

First published in 2011 by Barbour Publishing.
This edition published in 2020.

Copyright © 2011 by Debby Mayne

Recycling programs
for this product may
not exist in your area.

This edition published by arrangement with Harlequin Books S.A.

For questions and comments about the quality of this book,
please contact us at CustomerService@Harlequin.com.

Harlequin Enterprises ULC
22 Adelaide St. West, 40th Floor
Toronto, Ontario M5H 4E3, Canada
www.Harlequin.com

Printed in U.S.A.

TRUSTING
HER HEART

Chapter One

Mary Penner Glick's gaze darted to something behind Shelley, and a grin twitched the corners of her lips. "Guess who's walking in the door now."

Shelley Burkholder spun around as Jeremiah Yoder scanned the near-empty restaurant. The breakfast crowd at the small diner had dwindled, and the lunch crowd hadn't arrived yet. Her pulse quickened at the sight of Jeremiah, but she froze in place.

"Want me to seat him and take his order?" Mary offered.

"No, that's not necessary. You need to run along. I'm sure Abe doesn't want to be kept waiting."

The sound of Mary's laughter rang as she firmly placed her hand on Shelley's shoulder. "I miss working here, so it's my pleasure. Take a minute to gather your thoughts, and I'll make sure everyone is taken care of."

Ever since Peter had surprised Shelley with an announcement that he was engaged to someone else, she knew better than to let any man have even a sliver of her heart. Besides the hurt, the emotional investment took more time and energy than she had, so she saw this as a sign from God that she had no business falling in love anyway.

"Shelley, would you mind getting another pot of coffee brewing?" Joseph Penner called out, interrupting her thoughts.

"Sure, Mr. Penner." She scurried toward the beverage station.

Mary joined her as she poured the water into the coffeemaker well. "I just put Jeremiah's order in. Want me to stick around and deliver it when it's done, or can you handle him?" She reached up and adjusted her kapp, making Shelley smile.

Mary had always had a difficult time keeping her kapp on her head.

"No, no, run along. You've already done more than you should around here."

"If you're sure…" Mary took a step toward the door. "I'll check on you later to see how things go with Jeremiah."

Shelley forced a smile. "Stop worrying about me. I'll be fine. Jeremiah is the least of my concerns."

With a teasing glance, Mary chuckled. "Okay, if you say so." Shelley waited until Mary left the restaurant before sighing.

If Jeremiah hadn't been such a rebel, she might be flattered by his advances, which had started right after Mary and her husband, Abe, got married. But Jeremiah had left the Conservative Mennonite church once, and she wasn't sure he wouldn't do it again. Her child-hood crush on Jeremiah Yoder was part of her past and needed to stay that way—out of her present and future—if she wanted a peaceful life. Between her mother's recent mood dips and trying to help out with her younger brother, William, who had Down syndrome and a penchant for running away when he was upset, Shelley had little time for matters of the heart. Perhaps the Lord wanted her to stay single. It certainly seemed that way.

"Shelley, your order is up." Mr. Penner smiled. "Want me to bring it over to him?"

She inhaled deeply, squared her shoulders, and forced a smile. "I'll do it."

As she took the plate from the pass-through counter, Shelley said a silent prayer for the strength to face Jeremiah. If she hadn't been so attracted to him, waiting on him wouldn't be so difficult. And if he hadn't stayed away from the church for so long, none of this would matter. When he'd made it clear that he was interested in her, fear of losing her heart to the wrong man had forced her to erect a shield of protection.

Shelley carried the plate filled with eggs, ham, and biscuits over to the table where Jeremiah sat alone. "Here you go. Anything else I can get for you?"

He took a sip of his orange juice, set it on the table, and smiled at her, his light-brown eyes sparkling as they crinkled at the corners. "Some coffee would be good. Can you join me?"

"Neh." She hadn't meant the word to come out so

quickly and with such sharpness. "I mean, I can't sit down while I'm working."

"Don't you get a break?"

"*Ya*, but I already took it."

His lips formed a straight line as he nodded. "I understand. Maybe some other time."

"Maybe." She took a step back before adding, "I'll get your coffee. Want cream with that?"

"Yes, please." The gleam in his eye made her tummy flutter. She went to the beverage station and poured some coffee into a carafe, but the cream pitcher was empty. Shelley scurried toward the kitchen to get some cream, happy for a chance to gather her thoughts. Jeremiah's politeness would be stifling if she didn't know him well. He'd always been such a tease for as long as she'd known him, from back before they'd even started school. They both grew up in the Pinecraft community of Sarasota, a neighborhood of small houses rented by Conservative Mennonite and Amish families. Jeremiah had left the church right after high school and decided not to come back after getting a taste of the outside world. From what she'd seen and heard, he'd completely turned his back on his faith during that time. And now he wanted to come back. Shelley wished she could be so sure of his intentions, but it happened too fast…and at a bad time for Shelley. She didn't think she could face more heartbreak so soon after Peter announced he was marrying someone else.

On her way to Jeremiah's table she grabbed a cup from the beverage station, and then she filled it with coffee at Jeremiah's table and set the carafe down next to it. "Let me know if you need anything else, okay?"

He nodded but didn't say another word.

Jeremiah watched Shelley as she directed customers to tables after they walked into the family-owned restaurant lined with booths on each side and rows of laminate-topped tables in the middle of the floor. There was very little decor in the dining area to pull his attention away from Shelley. She appeared self-conscious when he talked to her, but her grace and assuredness returned the instant she turned her back on him. No matter what he said or did to show how much he cared for her, she appeared to keep an emotional distance.

As she glided around with ease in her midcalf-length full skirt, he couldn't help but notice her graceful, fluid movement. The crocheted kapp perched atop her braided chestnut-brown bun showed off her long, elegant neckline, which was devoid of any jewelry. Yes, he was physically attracted to her, but Jeremiah knew her heart was right with God. That alone compelled him to be near her, particularly at this time of his life as he prayed for forgiveness and mercy. One of the many people who hadn't accepted Jeremiah when he first came back was Shelley, but she was the one he really wanted to be happy. When Jeremiah first went to Abe to ask for help in coming back to the church, he'd been surprised at the quick acceptance from Abe and a few of the other church members. Shelley seemed pleased at how he'd helped Abe protect Mary from a man who'd tried to harm her, but now she acted like he'd somehow hurt her.

Abe told him it would take some time to win her over, but to Jeremiah it seemed as though that may never happen. He'd been working with some of the other hands tearing down Abe's old barn to prevent another accident when Abe approached him and said to go pick up some things in town, since Jeremiah still had transportation. He'd traded in the shiny sports car he'd used to impress girls for a barely functional automobile that wouldn't impress anyone. And he'd donated his stylish clothes to a charity thrift store and embraced the plain wardrobe filled with neutral-tone trousers and shirts.

As Jeremiah was about to get into his car, Abe advised him to stop off at Penner's Restaurant for breakfast before returning, since they'd be working until sundown. What he suspected Abe wanted was for him to have some face time with Shelley. Now he wondered at the wisdom. Perhaps he needed to make himself scarce for a while, so she wouldn't get annoyed with him.

He stared down at his nearly empty plate. Ever since he'd started working on Abe's farm, his appetite had practically doubled.

"Can I get you something else?"

The sound of Shelley's sweet voice caught his attention. He slowly looked up and met her blue-eyed gaze to see her studying him with concern. He shook his head. "This is already more food than I'm used to."

Shelley nodded as she glanced at his plate. "*Ya*, I can imagine. How are you able to be away from the farm so long?"

Jeremiah had to stifle a smile. This was the most she'd chatted with him since Abe and Mary's wedding. "Abe told me to have a big breakfast while I'm in town picking up supplies."

"You still drive your car?"

"Yes."

The look of disapproval on her face told him more than words possibly could.

"So if you ever need a lift somewhere, just call me."

She shook her head. "I rarely have a need to ride in a car."

He held up both hands. "I'm just offering rides when you need them."

Shelley's long, dark eyelashes fluttered for a moment as she closed her eyes and then opened them, meeting his gaze. She smiled. "Thank you, Jeremiah. Let me know when you're ready for your bill. I have to go see about my other"—she glanced over her shoulder before turning back—"my other customer."

The other customer happened to be one of Shelley's regulars—Blake, a truck driver who stopped off at Penner's whenever he was in town. The first time she and Mary had seen Blake, they were frightened by the man's oversized arms and the multiple tattoos he didn't bother hiding. But he was polite and expressed his appreciation for what he called "good home-cooked food like Mama used to make, rest her soul." And he'd left a tip bigger than his bill.

"Hi there, Shelley. What's the lunch special today?"

"Meatloaf, but it's not ready yet. It should be done in just a few minutes."

"Okay, then I'll wait." He closed the menu, folded his arms, and leaned back in his booth. "Who's that guy staring at you?"

"Oh, that's just Jeremiah. He's an old classmate." Shelley tried to act nonchalant, but she didn't think she did a good job of pulling it off.

"Old classmate, huh?" Blake's laughter was deep and resonant. "Looks to me like he carries a torch for you." He wiggled his eyebrows. "Want me to make him jealous?"

Shelley hopped back from the table. "*Neh*, that wouldn't be good."

"Don't worry, honey, I'm not gonna hurt you. I might look tough, but that's just a front. In the line of work I do, I gotta have an image."

"I know that," Shelley said with a forced smile. "Would you like something to drink while you wait for lunch?"

"Yeah, I'll have some sweet tea."

As Shelley turned toward the beverage station, she caught Jeremiah glaring at her. Blake was right. He was clearly jealous! The look on his face was one she'd never seen on him before, but she recognized it from studying other people.

Jeremiah quickly shoved his plate away, took another swig of coffee, stood, and reached into his back pocket for his wallet. As soon as she delivered Blake's tea, she brought Jeremiah his bill. Shelley wasn't short at five-foot-seven, but Jeremiah's broad six-foot frame made her feel small. He handed her a ten-dollar bill and said, "Keep the change."

"Thank you."

He started toward the door but stopped and spun back around to face her. "When do you generally take a break?"

"It varies. Most of the time right after the breakfast crowd dwindles, but I still don't like to take too long."

"I'll remember that." With a nod, he left.

As soon as the lunch special was ready, Shelley served Blake and waited on customers as they trickled into the restaurant. Shortly after eleven they were fully staffed, so Shelley didn't have to cover the whole dining room by herself. By noon the place was packed and stayed that way for a solid hour and a half. After Mary had gotten married and moved out to the Glick farm with Abe, Mr. Penner had hired another waitress, Jocelyn. Shelley liked the girl, but she was a bit silly—even for an outsider. Mr. Penner told Jocelyn she wasn't allowed to dress in clothes that showed too much skin, so she wore short skirts over pants and tank tops over T-shirts. It took more convincing to get her to tone down her makeup, but after Mrs. Penner talked to her, Jocelyn instantly gave up her thick eyeliner and bloodred lipstick. Shelley didn't know what Mrs. Penner had said to Jocelyn, but it obviously worked.

"So what's kickin'?" Jocelyn asked once business slowed down.

"I beg your pardon?"

"Anything new happenin' in your life?"

Shelley slowly shook her head. "No, not much that I can think of. Everything pretty much stays the same for me." Even if something were happening, Shelley couldn't imagine sharing it with someone like Jocelyn.

"I've got some great news I'm bustin' to tell someone." She grinned. "My sister is pregnant with twins."

"You have a sister?"

"Well, half sister. My mom had her after she left me and Dad."

"Oh, um…" Shelley wasn't sure what to say or how to react.

Jocelyn smiled. "She contacted me a few years ago, and we've started getting close."

"That's very good news," Shelley agreed. "Children are such a blessing in a marriage."

"Oh, my sister isn't married. She's not sure she's ready to settle down."

Shelley let out a gasp. "But why—" She stopped herself from asking what she considered the obvious.

"Oh, I know how you people feel about that, but I thought you'd at least be happy I'm gonna be an aunt."

"I'm sure you'll enjoy them very much." Shelley scurried toward the door to seat some late-arriving customers.

Things had changed around Pinecraft, and Shelley found it quite unsettling. In the past, Mr. Penner would never have hired anyone who wasn't Mennonite or Amish. But as people moved away or left the church, he'd been forced to bring in outsiders to help out. Even so, not many people were lined up for jobs, so he had to accept anyone who had the slightest bit of experience. His wife said they'd be better off shorthanded, but as good as Shelley was, she couldn't handle the restaurant alone during the busiest of times. At least Mrs. Penner came around to check on things more frequently now. Mr. Penner had a soft spot in his heart for the down-trodden, regardless of their faith or lack of it. Jocelyn had been unemployed for a long time, and when she'd told him she was a week away from living on the street because her dad wasn't able to support her anymore, he gave her the job.

It was late spring, and the temperatures were rising but hadn't reached the nineties yet. The winter visitors, also called snowbirds, had gone home, so the highways and businesses weren't nearly as crowded as they were as little as a month ago. The Pinecraft community in Sarasota played host to Amish and Mennonite visitors who preferred the mild winters in Florida over wher-ever they came from. Many of them stayed with rela-tives who lived in the tiny rental houses, while others had short-term leases of their own for the season.

As Jeremiah drove down the long, narrow, shell-covered driveway toward the Glick farm, he spotted Abe standing outside the old barn with a couple of the other workers. Jonathan Polk and his adult son,

Charles, were part of the crew Abe had put together from a group of farmhands to take down the barn.

Abe lifted a hand in greeting, but he continued talking. One of the things Jeremiah appreciated about his friend and boss was his no-nonsense approach to everything he did. There was never any guessing or wondering where he stood. If Abe said something, that was exactly what he meant.

Jeremiah opened the trunk of his old black car and pulled out some of the supplies for the farm. By the time he'd set everything down, Abe had sent the other men off to do their chores, and he'd joined Jeremiah.

"Did you stop by Penner's?" he asked.

"Yes, but Shelley still seems distant."

Abe shook his head. "Give her some time. After your behavior in the past, I can understand her reluctance."

"Don't forget, Abe, I helped you with that bad dude, Jimbo, when he came after Mary. Shelley was there, so she knows I helped."

Abe tilted his head forward and gave Jeremiah a stern glare. "I'm sure Shelley is well aware of your good deeds, but you need to remember to exercise some humility. Don't boast about what you do because you want people to notice. The Lord sees everything, and He's the only one whose judgment matters."

Jeremiah lowered his head. "Yeah, you're right. I'm still struggling with some things."

"Don't put too much pressure on yourself or rush

your relationship with Shelley. Let the Lord do His work in His own time."

"Thanks, Abe." Jeremiah turned toward the pile of supplies. "I'll go get the wheelbarrow, so I can bring this stuff in one load."

Abe placed a hand on Jeremiah's shoulder. "Trust that Shelley will eventually come around and see what a good man you are and that you've left those unruly years behind." He paused before adding, "That is, if it's the Lord's will."

Jeremiah nodded.

For the next couple of hours as Jeremiah worked with his hands, he allowed himself to reflect on his past. Abe was right. The acts he'd committed during the years that he had spent away from the church needed quite a bit of forgiving. He'd fallen into the trap of chasing the wrong kind of women, pursuing more material objects than he'd ever need in a lifetime, and being the kind of man who'd frighten someone like Shelley. In his own mind at the time, he'd managed to place some of the blame for his indiscretions on Shelley. He'd had a crush on her since they were teenagers, but she never had time for him. She was always running home saying she needed to help her mother and younger brother. At the time, he saw it as a personal rejection, but now he knew she was being an obedient daughter.

Shelley preferred walking over riding the three-wheeler around the community as so many of the other neighbors did. Her adult-sized tricycle stayed tethered to the pole in the carport unless she needed it to haul groceries or other items from the store. Since she worked the early-morning shift, she generally went home after the last of the lunch customers left.

As she rounded the last corner toward the house her family rented, she slowed down and said a prayer that she'd find her mother in a better mood than when she'd left. Ever since her younger brother, William, was born with Down syndrome, her mother suffered from depression, and her father retreated further into silence when he wasn't working. When William got upset, he liked to be alone, so sometimes he took off without telling anyone where he was going, which upset their mother even more. Her older brother, Paul, left the church as soon as he was old enough to find a job to support himself. At first their parents were so disappointed they didn't want him coming around, in case Shelley might get ideas to do the same. After he and his wife had their first child, the allure of grandparenting had been so strong that they'd accepted him and his family with the hope that Paul would return to the church and bring his family with him. Paul's wife, Tammy, had a sweet disposition, and Shelley adored her niece, Lucy, and nephew, Grady. Shelley wondered if she'd ever have children of her own someday, but as time passed, she wondered if most men wouldn't want to take a wife who'd ultimately wind up with the responsibility of a mentally challenged brother who would need care for the rest of his life. If Paul had stayed with the church, he would have taken William in, but Shelley was the only option. Until Peter let her down, Shelley had thought there might've been hope, but now she'd settled back to her old way of thinking.

The side door by the carport was unlocked. As she entered the house, the eerie silence disturbed her. William went to school and then an afternoon group work session during the week, and he wouldn't be home until the van dropped him off right before dinner. A single dinner plate and a glass were in the sink, letting Shelley know her mother had eaten alone. Her father had tried to talk her mother into getting a part-time job, just to get her out of the house and more socially active, but she'd insisted she needed to be home in case William needed her. She set the takeout box filled with cake on the counter before leaving the kitchen.

"Mother," Shelley called out. "Are you home?"

She was met by silence, so she made her way through the tiny three-bedroom house, glancing in each room, praying her mother would be awake. When she got to the nearly dark master bedroom, she saw movement in the bed. Recently, her mother had started napping and waking up after Shelley got home from work.

"What time is it?" her mother asked. "I didn't mean to sleep so late."

"It's a little past two."

Mother sat up in bed and patted the hair that had come loose from her bun. "Oh, good. I've only been asleep for an hour." She shoved her feet into the clogs by the bed and slowly stood. Shelley couldn't help but notice her mother grabbing onto the nightstand for support.

"If you're not feeling well, why don't you lie back down?" Shelley said. "I can finish the chores."

"There isn't much to do, since I'm the only person here all morning."

Shelley was exhausted from the busy morning at Penner's, but she thought about her father's attempts to cheer up her mother and decided she should at least try to advance his cause. "Would you like to take a walk with me now?"

"Isn't it awful hot to be walking?"

"The rain last night cooled things down a bit, so it's not too bad. We can just stroll around the block and get some fresh air."

Her mother's hesitation let her know she didn't want to do it, but she couldn't think of a good enough reason. Finally, she sighed and nodded. "Okay, but just around the block."

"I'll put a few things away while you get ready," Shelley offered. "Mr. Penner sent me home with some dessert. He said he and Mrs. Penner haven't been eating as many sweets since Mary got married and moved out."

"Just give me a few minutes, and I'll join you in the kitchen." Shelley left her mother alone to do whatever she needed to get ready for their walk. She put her tote on the hook in her room and then went to the kitchen and put the cake in the refrigerator so the cream-cheese icing wouldn't spoil. Then she washed the dishes in the sink and wiped the crumbs off the table.

"I'm ready."

Shelley glanced up and spotted her mother at the door wearing a different skirt and some hard-soled shoes. "Don't you want to wear comfortable shoes?" Shelley asked.

"*Neh*, these are fine. I'm used to them."

Shelley had her doubts, but she didn't push. Her mother grabbed the key off the hook, and they took off.

"Anything interesting happen at work today?" Shelley's mother asked.

Shelley pondered mentioning Jeremiah but made a quick decision not to. "No, pretty much a normal day."

"I had a visitor this morning, shortly after William went to school."

When her mother didn't continue, Shelley slowed her pace and turned to look at her mother. "Well? Who was it?"

"Hannah."

Peter's mother. The downside to growing up in a community where everyone knew everyone else made it difficult getting over the man she once thought she'd marry. "Did she say anything I need to know about?"

Her mother shrugged. "She doesn't know if Peter is happy."

"What gives her that impression?"

"He seems restless."

Despite the fact that Shelley had thought she was madly in love with Peter before he'd informed her he was marrying someone else, she'd gotten over him. "I think Peter's always restless," Shelley said.

"Hannah seems to think Peter regrets his decision and that he's considering calling off his wedding."

If there had been any doubt about things turning out for the best in Shelley's life, it was gone. After the breakup, she'd realized that Peter always wondered what he was missing, and he was seldom satisfied with what he had.

"He might just be holding a torch for you."

"I don't think so," Shelley said.

"You wouldn't know though, would you?"

"Mother, even if Peter wants me back, I don't think we're meant for each other."

"You're not getting any younger, Shelley. I don't want you to miss out on a chance of finding a suitable husband. Peter is a good man, and if he wants to reconsider his decision, you should—"

"No, I shouldn't. I don't love Peter."

Her mother frowned. "Peter will be a good provider, and you know him very well."

"Not as well as I once thought."

"You should give him another chance."

"Considering the fact that he hasn't asked for another chance, that's a moot point," Shelley said. She noticed that they'd slowed way down. "Are you okay, Mother?"

"My feet are tired."

Shelley stopped. "Why don't you take off your shoes and walk barefoot?"

"I'll give that a try for a little while." She placed her hand on Shelley's shoulder to steady herself as she took off each shoe with the other hand. "Now what were we talking about?" Silence fell between them for a few seconds. "Oh, Peter. So would you like me to ask his mother if he might want to stop by the house soon?"

Had Mother not heard a single word she'd said? "I'm not interested in Peter anymore." Shelley turned and started walking again. Traffic had begun to pick up, so she had to wait at the corner before crossing. A black automobile slowed as it approached, and she glanced at the driver—Jeremiah.

The car stopped, and Jeremiah waved. "Hey, Shelley. Mrs. Burkholder. Want a ride somewhere?"

If Shelley had been alone, she would have turned him down, but her mother's feet were hurting. "Mother?"

Her mother audibly sighed and then nodded. "Yes, I think a ride would be very nice."

Chapter Two

Jeremiah wasn't sure what just happened, but he had to smile. One minute he was driving home from work, and the next minute he spotted Shelley and her mother walking down the street. Mrs. Burkholder had been limping. He'd stopped with the intention of offering a ride, but he wasn't sure they'd take him up on it. He was surprised when they accepted. Shelley's mother got into the front seat next to him, and Shelley slid into the backseat.

"Where to, ladies?"

"Home, please," Shelley said.

Jeremiah tried to make small talk as they drove to the Burkholder house. He could tell they were both uncomfortable, so he decided to take a low-key approach.

"Nice day for a walk," he said.

Mrs. Burkholder cleared her throat but didn't say anything. He glanced in the rearview mirror and saw a pained expression on Shelley's face. She mouthed, "I'm sorry."

Okay, so conversation would be rough. At least their house wasn't too far. As soon as he brought the car to a complete stop, Mrs. Burkholder unbuckled her seat belt, flung open the door, and jumped out. She glanced over her shoulder and scowled at Shelley before darting into the house, leaving Jeremiah and Shelley alone.

"I guess I came along at the right time, huh?" Jeremiah said.

"I guess you did. You do realize the only reason I got in your car with you was because my mother's feet hurt."

So that explained the limp. "Then I'm glad I came along when I did."

Shelley nodded. "*Ya*, your timing was good."

She remained in the car, so he pondered for a few seconds whether or not he should take advantage of the situation. Might as well, he thought. "Would you like to go out with me sometime?"

"I don't think so," she said. "You should know that by now."

"I was hoping you'd changed your mind about me."

"What makes you think I'd ever change my mind?"

"C'mon, Shelley. I was young and restless, but that's in my past. You know I see things differently now. I've turned my life back over to the Lord."

"What's to say you won't change your mind again?"

Jeremiah challenged her with a firm gaze in the mirror. "What's to say you won't do what I did?"

"Well," she began as she reached for the door handle. "I don't have the history you have. Even before you left, you were somewhat of a rebel."

"Yeah, I'll give you that."

"People don't change." She opened the door, but she didn't get out yet.

"Not unless the Lord chooses to change them," Jeremiah countered. "What can I do to prove to you that my heart is right with the Lord?"

"I'm not the one you have to prove anything to."

"I know that, but I want you to see that I've returned to my faith. And I want you to believe it as well." He glanced up and spotted her mother peeking around from behind the drapes. "Someone's watching us."

She pushed the car door all the way open and started to get out before turning back to face Jeremiah. "I'm happy you came back to the church, Jeremiah, but only for you. It has nothing to do with me."

"You're right. It's all about the Lord's direction. He's in charge of my life now, and I want to serve Him well."

Shelley finally cracked a smile. "I hope that's truly the way it is. We'll see how things go when you start to get restless again. But now I better go inside. I'm sure my mother has plenty to say about me sitting here with you."

"I'll see you soon, Shelley."

She got out and slammed the car door shut. Jeremiah sat and waited until she was safely inside her house.

As Shelley walked inside, she was surprised her mother wasn't standing by the door waiting for her with a long lecture, but instead she was met by silence, which brought confusion and worry. Her mother seemed more fragile recently, so she tried very hard—most of the time—not to upset her.

She sighed and went into the kitchen to start supper. As tired as she was after working such a busy shift, walking with her mother, and talking to Jeremiah, she knew that her father and William would be hungry when they got home. William liked to set the table, but her father expected to sit right down to a big meal after a long day working at the hardware store.

She'd just placed the pork chops into the oven when she saw a shadow by the door. She turned around and offered her mother a guarded smile.

"What did you and Jeremiah talk about?"

Shelley shrugged. "Not much. He just wanted to remind me that he's changed."

"Just remember, Shelley, the temptations of evil are powerful."

It took everything Shelley had not to roll her eyes. "Nothing evil happened. Jeremiah was actually very sweet to stop and pick us up."

"That's how it starts."

Shelley let out a deep sigh. Even after Jeremiah had saved her mother from having to walk back home with aching feet, she still hadn't softened. "Look, Mother, I'm not going to do anything I shouldn't do. Jeremiah says he's committed his life to the Lord, and from my perspective, it appears that he has."

Even though Shelley rarely outwardly rebelled, she

wasn't about to openly admit her own doubts about Jeremiah.

Silence fell between them for a moment. Shelley felt as though the conversation didn't stand a chance of having any resolution, so she thought it best to end the discussion. Her mother apparently thought otherwise.

"So you're saying that you don't have any doubts about Jeremiah's motives on coming around again?"

"No, I'm not saying that." Deep down, Shelley feared that what her mother was saying was true, and she would have been on her mother's side if she'd been talking to Jeremiah. But when he looked at her as he had a half hour ago, she wanted to believe him, even though she wouldn't let him know. "I just think we need to give him the benefit of proving himself."

"Shelley, you can be so naive."

"He helped Abe when that awful man came to hurt Mary," Shelley reminded her mother.

"Don't base your opinion of him on a few good deeds. He was away from the church for a number of years, and it'll take much more than that to show he's changed for the good."

Shelley didn't have an argument for that, so she finally backed away. "We need to finish preparing supper so Father and William have something to eat when they come home."

The cloud of their conversation hung over them as they finished cooking. By the time William walked through the door, Shelley was exhausted more from what wasn't being said than from what was.

"Can you take me to the park before supper?" William asked.

"Not now," Shelley replied. "I'm busy."

William's face scrunched into a pout. He opened his mouth to say something, but Shelley noticed their mother giving him a look that stopped him.

Shelley wished Mother would give William a little more room to explore on his own. After all, he was seventeen. But unless he was at school, work, or in the van that took him to work, Mother insisted someone from the family be with him.

Jeremiah appreciated the physical labor of farm work. It enabled him to reflect on not only his conversation with Shelley two days ago but also conversations he'd had with some of the church elders over the past several months since he'd come back to his Mennonite roots. He was constantly being questioned about his motives and why he'd chosen this time to come back to the church. The reasons didn't seem clear, although he had no doubt that the Lord sometimes painfully taught him lessons that steered him back. He explained that to Abe, who seemed to understand, but his answers didn't satisfy everyone.

The people who never questioned him were Jonathan and his son, Charles, a couple of outsiders Abe hired to help out on the farm. Jeremiah enjoyed working with them.

"Watch out, Jeremiah," Jonathan said with a teasing tone. "A man who thinks too much can get hurt."

Jeremiah chuckled. "You're right. I've been think-ing too much lately."

"Care to talk about it?" Jonathan raked his fingers through his half-gray, half-brown hair. "Not saying I have all the answers, but sometimes it helps to talk."

"If I had any idea what to talk about, I'd probably welcome the opportunity, but my thoughts are so jum-bled they don't even make sense to me."

Jonathan nodded his understanding. "I know exactly what you're saying. This world is confusing, which is why I brought my son here to learn what's really im-portant."

Jeremiah glanced over at Jonathan's son, Charles, who was busy hauling lumber from the old barn to the scrap pile. "Charles seems to be in his element here on the farm."

"He and I are both much happier than we've ever been. No high-powered executive job has ever left me with the sense of accomplishment that I get from work-ing here."

"I know what you mean."

"Yes," Jonathan said with a nod. "I know you do. And one of these days, others will see that in you. Some people just need to get burned a few times before we come to our senses."

"That's a good way of putting it. I needed to get burned before I understood what I had. And now I want that back. The Lord's favor is all that matters to me right now."

"It's okay to want the girl, too," Jonathan said.

Jeremiah grinned. "Am I that obvious?"

"Yes, you definitely are. Any chance you'll be letting go of the car?"

"Abe and I have been talking about it. I already traded in my sports car for the plain one, but it's hard to give up transportation."

"I know what you mean. Charles and I have been talking about that. He seems more amenable to it than I am, but if I ever decide to embrace the lifestyle, it seems the right thing to do. My wife isn't ready yet, but she seems happier already now that we've decided to try and sell the house."

The clanging sound of the triangle signaling lunchtime got their attention. "I'm starving," Jeremiah said as he patted his belly. "Another cool thing about working here is being able to eat anything I want and not having to worry about an expanding waistline. It seemed like no matter how much time I spent at the gym before, I always had to loosen my belt a notch or two after a big meal."

After they finished the bag lunches they'd brought from home, Abe approached Jeremiah. "Do you mind taking me to town? I have to deliver some produce to Penner's."

"I'll be glad to."

"I thought you might." Abe turned to Jonathan. "Tell your wife we enjoyed her pineapple upside-down cake. Mary would like the recipe."

"Lori will be flattered," Jonathan said. "I'll have her jot down the recipe."

Abe gave a clipped nod. "Good. Jeremiah, let me know when you're ready to go."

Jeremiah finished the last of his sandwich and rose from the picnic bench. "Time to take the boss to town."

"I'll save some of the work for you when you get back," Jonathan said as he stood. "Drive carefully."

As soon as Abe got into Jeremiah's car, he started talking. "I heard you created quite a stir in town on Monday."

Jeremiah frowned as he reflected. He didn't know what Abe was talking about. "I did?"

"*Ya.* Shelley's mother was very unhappy about you showing up."

"Oh, that. Well, I didn't mean to cause any trouble. It's just that I saw Shelley and her mother walking, so I thought I'd offer them a ride."

"Just remember that it takes a while to earn forgiveness from people who have been hurt. When you left, you upset some folks."

"That wasn't my intention."

"It doesn't have to be. It just happens that way sometimes."

When Jeremiah had to stop for a light, he turned to Abe. "What can I do to make things better?"

"If you're asking how you can hurry things along, I don't have any answers. But if you want to make amends with individual people, you can talk to them and explain your reasons for coming back. They need to know you have no motive other than to please the Lord and do His calling."

Jeremiah wished it were that simple, but he knew it wasn't. He'd always cared for Shelley, but she'd always seemed leery of him even when they were younger. That's why he'd been surprised when she'd gotten into his car on Monday.

"If you want to court Shelley, you need to make things right with her parents first."

"I doubt they'll bother talking to me," Jeremiah said.

"Have you tried?"

"No."

"Then do that first. You knew coming back wouldn't be easy."

"True." Jeremiah accelerated as the light turned green. "Something I've been wondering, Abe."

"What's that?"

"You didn't put me through the paces when I wanted to come back. Everyone else has one question after another, but you accepted what I said from the get-go. Why was that?"

Abe shrugged. "I s'pose I've always been a direct sort of man, and I've known you to be that way with me. There wasn't any reason for me to doubt you— particularly after you swallowed your pride when I talked to you about your crudeness with Mary."

Jeremiah cringed as he remembered his comments. "That was totally out of line. The second I hollered at you, I regretted it. I'm afraid I picked up some bad habits."

"But you apologized, and you seemed sincere. Mary and I have both forgiven you."

"Now I need to ask a lot of other people for their forgiveness."

"*Ya.* That's exactly what you have to do. Some people will accept your words, and others will wait and watch your actions."

"That's a lot of pressure."

"Pressure is part of life," Abe said. "After you establish yourself back in the church, there will be something else. Walking with the Lord isn't easy for anyone."

"How about you, Abe? Do you feel pressure about anything?"

"*Ya,* of course I do. But I don't lose sleep over it. Mary and I pray about whatever is on our minds, and we go to sleep knowing we're in the Lord's good graces. As Christians, we are His faithful servants, even when we slip up. He has never let us down."

That was exactly what Jeremiah needed to hear. He helped Abe unload the produce from the trunk, and then Joseph Penner asked them to stick around. Abe accepted, but Jeremiah asked if he could run an errand of his own. Abe smiled knowingly and nodded.

On the way to the Burkholders' house, Jeremiah prayed for the Lord's mercy and for the wisdom to say the right thing to Shelley's mother. Pride had always been a problem for Jeremiah, but he knew the Lord was working on that.

He pulled up in front of the Burkholders' house, stopped, and said a prayer for guidance. His hands were damp and a little shaky as he got out of the car and walked up to the front door. After a brief pause, he knocked.

The silence gave him the impression no one was home, so he turned to leave. The sound of the door opening behind him caught his attention. He turned around and saw Mrs. Burkholder glaring at him.

"What do you want, Jeremiah?"

"I'd like to talk to you, if you're not too busy."

The woman tightened her jaw and narrowed her eyes. "Shelley isn't here right now."

"I know. That's why I came. I'd like to talk to you alone."

She continued to scrutinize him, making him feel small and weak. Finally, she nodded. "I suppose you can come in, but not for long. I have chores to do."

Grateful for an opportunity to talk to Shelley's mother, Jeremiah followed the woman into her tidy little house, which was almost the exact same layout as the one he'd grown up in. She led him to the kitchen, which overlooked an equally well-kept backyard.

"Would you like some coffee?" she asked.

"No, thank you." He gestured toward the kitchen table. "Mind if we sit?"

She looked at the table and then took a step toward the chair. "I hope you realize I'm not in favor of you seeing my daughter."

"Yes, I'm aware of that, but I'd like to find out if there's anything I can do to prove myself."

"You've already proven yourself, Jeremiah, and I don't mean that in a good way."

"I'm working hard now, Mrs. Burkholder. Abe has given me a job on his farm, and I'm back in the church now. What else can I do to show you I'm sincerely repentant of my indiscretions?"

She pursed her lips and shook her head. "I don't think there's anything you can do for my husband and me to give you our blessing to see our daughter."

That was what Jeremiah had been afraid of. He hung his head and sent up a prayer. Finally, after a few more minutes of quiet, he stood. "I better go pick Abe up from the restaurant. I told him I wouldn't be long."

"You know your way out," Mrs. Burkholder said.

He nodded and turned to leave when the sound of someone knocking at the door echoed through the house. Mrs. Burkholder jumped to her feet and ran along behind him.

When Jeremiah opened the door, he found himself face-to-face with a sheriff's deputy. "Officer," he said in greeting.

The deputy leaned around Jeremiah. "Mrs. Burkholder, we just got a call that your son, William, has wandered off from the school. A deputy has been dispatched to search the area, but I wanted to let you know."

"I'll help," Jeremiah said without a moment's hesitation. "I'll go get Abe, and we'll get right to work."

Mrs. Burkholder was right behind him. "I'm coming with you."

The officer stepped up. "Someone needs to stay here in case William comes home."

Jeremiah looked at the woman, who now looked frail.

"Why don't you wait here? I have the car, so we can cover a larger area."

Her forehead crinkled in concern, and she nodded. "I don't have any way of communicating."

Jeremiah pulled the cell phone out of his pocket and handed it to her. "I'll find a phone and call you if— when—we find him."

She hesitated before nodding and accepting the phone. "If I don't hear from you soon, I'll walk over to Penner's."

"Please stay right here, ma'am," the deputy advised. "Someone needs to be home if he decides to return on his own."

Jeremiah scooted past the deputy and ran out to his car. By the time he arrived at Penner's, another deputy had stopped by and made Abe, Mr. Penner, and Shelley aware of what had happened. Shelley was beside herself.

"Any idea where he might have gone?" he asked Shelley.

"He wanders from home sometimes," Shelley replied. "But I can't imagine why he left the school. He loves his teacher. I'm worried that something terrible has happened to him. Someone needs to let my father know."

The deputy nodded. "We've sent someone to his workplace to tell him."

Jeremiah shook his head. "I have a feeling we'll

find him, but we shouldn't wait too long. Why don't you come with me?"

Shelley turned to Mr. Penner, who nodded. "Okay."

"Oh, I gave your mother my cell phone, so I'll need a way to stay in touch."

Shelley reached into her apron pocket and pulled out a phone. "I have mine."

"Then let's go. We don't need to waste any time."

Jeremiah and Shelley ran out to Jeremiah's car. "Let's swing by the school and drive around the block. We can widen our search as we go."

She swallowed hard and nodded. "My little brother is so trusting. I sure hope he didn't go off with someone."

"Who would he go off with?"

Shelley shrugged. "Maybe someone offered him something he wanted."

"How old is William now?"

"Seventeen," she replied. "Almost eighteen."

"It's not like he's a little boy someone would want to abduct. He's almost as tall as me, and he looks strong, so I doubt anyone could force him to do anything."

"*Ya*, he's very strong."

"Then let's not worry. We'll find him."

There was no activity in the school yard. "Looks like the teachers are keeping the kids inside." Jeremiah circled the block then turned down another street to widen their search. "Any thoughts about where he might be?"

Shelley tapped her chin with her index finger. "He loves ice cream, so he might have gone to one of the ice cream shops."

"Does he know how to find them?"

"I'm not sure. One of us is usually with him."

"Let's check out Slater's Creamery. That's the closest to the school."

"Good idea," Shelley said. "He likes their vanilla bean." Jeremiah pulled up in front and waited in the car while Shelley ran inside to ask if anyone had seen William. Hope welled inside him until she came back to the car shaking her head. "*Neh*, they said they haven't seen him since we were there last week."

Jeremiah drove to a few more places Shelley suggested, but they continued turning up empty. "He can't have gone very far since he's on foot."

Shelley's chin quivered. "But what if he's not on foot? What if he got into someone's automobile?"

"He wouldn't do that, would he?" Jeremiah asked as he continued driving slowly and looking down the side streets. "I mean, you and your parents have taught him it's not safe to wander off with strangers, right?"

"Of course, but he's still so trusting. William is one of the sweetest people in the world, so if someone said the right thing, he might have gone off with them."

Jeremiah pulled over to the curb. "Before we go on, let's say a prayer."

Shelley nodded as a tear trickled down her chin. Jeremiah put the car into *Park* and took hold of both of her hands. He prayed for William's safety and that he'd be found soon so everyone could stop worrying. After he said, "Amen," he opened his eyes and saw

Shelley staring at him. Shortly after their gazes met, she lowered her head.

He reached out and tucked his finger beneath her chin. "Shelley, I want to be there for you—now and after we find William. Will you at least give me a chance?"

She opened her mouth but quickly closed it. A few seconds later she said, "I don't know, Jeremiah. Everything is so confusing right now. All I can think about is finding my little brother."

Yes, of course. What had Jeremiah been thinking? He wanted to kick himself in the backside for being selfish enough to turn things around to his feelings for Shelley.

"I'm sorry, Shelley. My timing was off. I just want you to know how much I care and that I have confidence we'll find William."

"What if we don't this time?" she asked, fear evident in her expression.

"We will." He took her hand and squeezed it. "We always do. We just have to trust the Lord."

Chapter Three

He'd driven a few hundred feet when Shelley's hand flew to her mouth. "I think I might know where he is. Turn here," she said, pointing to a narrow road to the right. "He has been asking me to take him to the park when he gets home from school lately, but I was always so busy."

As soon as the park came into view, Jeremiah spotted movement near the flower garden. "That looks like him over there."

"It is. Stop the car."

As soon as the car came to a stop, Shelley handed Jeremiah her cell phone, jumped out, and ran toward the boy. Jeremiah placed a call to his cell phone, which Mrs. Burkholder answered on the second ring.

"We found him," Jeremiah said. "He's at the park. Shelley is talking to him now. We'll bring him home in a few minutes."

"Praise the Lord," Mrs. Burkholder said breathlessly. "I'll let my husband know."

"I'll call the police now," Jeremiah offered. "Then I'll call Abe, and he can tell the others."

"What are you doing here, William?" Shelley asked as she approached her younger brother. "Everyone is so worried about you."

William frowned before turning to pick another flower to add to the fistful he had in his left hand. "Mother is so sad. Pretty flowers will cheer her up."

"I'm sure they will, but why didn't you wait until I could bring you here?"

"I've been telling you I wanted to come here, but you never have time." William leaned toward another cluster of flowers. "Look at those purple flowers, Shelley. Aren't they pretty?"

"Yes, they're very pretty, but you need to come with me right now."

"But I want to pick more flowers to make Mother happy." His eyes brightened as he looked at something behind Shelley. "Hi, Jeremiah. Look at the pretty flowers I picked for my mother."

"Very nice," Jeremiah said. "Your mother will be very happy to see you…and the flowers. Are you ready to go home now?"

William plucked one more bloom then walked toward Jeremiah. "I don't want to be late for work, but I can't remember how to get back to school where they pick me up."

"I'll take you to work," Jeremiah offered.

"Oh, I don't think you need to worry about work

today," Shelley said. "You'll need to stay home after scaring Mother like you did."

A look of alarm came over William. "Did something happen to Mother?"

Shelley glanced at Jeremiah, who offered her a comforting smile. "Yes, William, something terrible happened to Mother. She thought she'd lost her youngest child. You scared her and us half out of our minds by taking off like that."

"Was I bad?"

Before Shelley had a chance to respond, Jeremiah spoke up. "No, William, you weren't bad. But you should always tell someone where you're going before you leave. People worry when they don't know where you are."

William hung his head. "I'm sorry."

"Come on, William. Let's get you home to Mother. She's waiting for you."

Shelley started to buckle William into the front seat with Jeremiah. He scowled at her. "I can buckle my own seat belt," he said. "Stop treating me like a baby."

Shelley let go of the seat belt and got in behind him. As they drove toward home, she listened to the conversation between the two men and marveled at how sensitive Jeremiah was. She'd seen brief glimpses of this with Jeremiah in the past, but just when she'd thought he had a sweet side, he'd do something to quickly erase that impression. Now she waited for it to happen again.

He pulled up in front of the house, turned off the car, and came around to help with William. Mother came running outside, and the instant William was all the way out of the car, she flung her arms around him, alternately kissing his face and fussing at him for taking off without telling anyone. Jeremiah stood to the side, watching and waiting—for what, she wasn't sure. When they looked at each other, he tilted his head forward in acknowledgment, but he still didn't say a word. She felt a flutter of something inside, but she wasn't about to let this emotion-charged moment affect her thoughts.

"Thank you for helping, Jeremiah," she said. "Mother, if it weren't for Jeremiah, William wouldn't be standing here right now."

"Well…" Mother's lips formed a straight line, and she clearly didn't know what to say or do.

Jeremiah lifted a hand in a wave. "I need to get back to work. I'm glad I could help. If you need anything, let me know."

He'd gotten into his car and started it when Shelley's mother spun and ran toward him. Shelley thought perhaps she wanted to thank him, but instead she held up a cell phone. "Don't forget this."

"Do you want to use it for a while?" he asked.

Her mother shook her head. "No, I prefer not having the intrusion, but I've decided I need to get my own."

Shelley was disappointed that her mother didn't thank Jeremiah for the phone, but she knew better than to say anything. Her relationship with her mother had been somewhat strained during the past several months. She wasn't sure why, but her mother seemed to be sad all the time—until now.

"You had us worried sick," Mother said over and over. "William, don't ever run off like that again."

William innocently held up the bouquet he still gripped, several of the more fragile blooms drooping. "I wanted to pick you some pretty flowers to cheer you up," he said. "When you're sad, I feel sad."

Mother accepted the flowers and placed them on the side table without a word. When it was obvious she wasn't going to do anything with them, Shelley picked up the bouquet. "I'll put them in some water. Aren't they pretty, Mother? William picked them just for you."

Still her mother said nothing. William appeared confused as he was ushered toward his room.

Shelley busied herself with cutting the bottoms of the stems and placing them in a glass they didn't use often. Her mother didn't keep vases because she said they were unnecessary and took up valuable space. The sparsely filled shelves could use something new, but her mother didn't believe in having anything around that wasn't used often. Although the plain life made sense, there was still room for something fun and interesting.

The house was so quiet Shelley could hear the low murmur of voices coming from the bedroom area. Her father had remained at work even though he was aware of what had happened. Shelley knew he was just as worried as the rest of them, so she wondered why he hadn't come home.

She puttered around the kitchen for a little while until finally her mother joined her. "William doesn't understand why I don't want him to go to work."

Shelley turned and faced her mother. "Why can't he?"

Her mother frowned. "Don't tell me you don't understand. He had me worried sick."

"But he's fine. I'm sure he understands that he shouldn't wander off like that now."

"I thought he knew that before." Mother closed her eyes and shook her head then let out a long-suffering sigh as she looked Shelley in the eye. "We can't take any more chances with him."

"What do you plan to do? Keep him home all the time?"

"If I have to."

Shelley lifted her eyebrows. "And what will that accomplish? Do you think the Lord wants you to live in fear like that all the time?"

"It's more out of protection than fear. If I know where he is at all times, I'll never have to worry."

"Oh, I'm sure you'll find something to worry about. You always do." The instant those words left Shelley's mouth, she regretted saying them.

"And what is that supposed to mean?"

"Mother, I know you love William. I love him, too. But he can't live in a bubble all his life. School and work are important to him. He has friends."

"He can see his friends at church."

Frustration washed over Shelley as she realized her

mother wasn't about to budge. "What will he do if you can't take care of him anymore?"

"That's where you come in," her mother replied. "Your father and I already thought about this before, and we decided that since Paul left, you're the logical person to care for your brother."

"Is that—" Shelley stopped herself before asking if that was why her mother was averse to her being around Jeremiah. Perhaps they thought she'd go off and leave William. She cleared her throat and started over. "You know I'll always be there for William no matter what, Lord willing."

"I certainly hope so."

"Jeremiah was very sweet for taking me to look for William. If he hadn't, I imagine it would have taken longer for us to find him."

"Just because Jeremiah happened to be here when William got lost…" Her mother's voice wandered off as she gazed out the window over the backyard.

Shelley studied her mother for a moment before speaking her mind. "Jeremiah was a big help, and I think we should be grateful that he jumped in and helped without having to be asked."

"I'd rather not discuss Jeremiah."

On Saturday the farmworkers finished taking down the last of the old barn. Now that Jeremiah was used to the manual labor, he was able to work without tiring as quickly as he had when he'd first come back. Since Abe was counseling him on issues related to the church, he hung around until everyone else had gone home.

"Seen Shelley lately?" Abe asked.

"Not since we found her brother and brought him home on Wednesday. Her mother still can't stand the sight of me."

Abe chuckled. "Mrs. Burkholder is a fair woman. I'm sure she'll eventually come around."

"Back when I was a betting man, I would have bet against that."

"Good thing you're no longer a betting man."

Jeremiah nodded. "I have some things I'd like to discuss with you."

"About Shelley?"

"We can talk about Shelley, but there's something else that's bothering me."

Abe gestured toward a chair on his porch. "Have a seat, and let's talk."

Once they sat down, Jeremiah opened up. "Before I decided to come back to the church, I did some things that I'm not proud of."

"*Ya*, I know that."

"There are some things you don't know."

Abe turned and looked at him, waiting patiently in silence.

"I took out some big loans that will take years to pay back."

"You are a hard worker, and you live with your parents," Abe said. "You'll pay those loans back in due time."

"There's more." Jeremiah hated sharing everything,

but he needed to come clean rather than have Abe find out later. "One of the men I worked with said some unsavory things about a woman I was dating, and I"—Jeremiah sucked in a deep breath—"I punched his lights out."

Abe tilted his head. "What do you mean by that?"

"I decked him." Jeremiah paused before clarifying. "I hit him with my fist."

"That is not good."

"And I spent three days in jail for unruly conduct."

Abe shook his head. "I hope the man you hit wasn't seriously injured."

"I broke his nose, which is why he pressed charges. Going to jail got me fired from my job, but I found another one."

"You need to ask the Lord for His forgiveness before you can move on."

"I've asked over and over, but I can't stop worrying about what happened."

Abe looked out over his land then turned back to Jeremiah and leaned forward with his elbows on his knees. "You need to trust that the Lord has forgiven you and move on. If He knows that you have sincere repentance for what you did, He will forgive you. From now on, you are to live as a peaceful man who will do no harm to anyone."

"That's what I intend to do," Jeremiah said. "But what if Shelley and her parents find out?"

"They will come to understand that is part of your

past," Abe said, "and that you are very sorry it happened."

"If they know about my past, do you think they will they ever trust me?"

Abe shrugged. "Best leave that up to the Lord. He's the only one who can bring forgiveness."

"So let's say they can't forgive me."

Abe lifted his eyebrows and nodded. "That's a possibility."

Jeremiah knew that Abe was right, but the thought of having Shelley turn her back on him for something he couldn't change stabbed him in the heart. "I want Shelley to see that I'm the kind of man who will love her and be there for her."

"Have you shown that yet?"

"I'm working on it. Like when I helped her find William."

"Just make sure you are doing things for the right reasons and not for some reward, like earning Shelley's love. She should love you for who you are rather than what you can do for her."

Abe's wisdom belied his years. No wonder he managed to prosper during times when so many others failed.

"Thanks, man. You really know your stuff."

Abe laughed out loud—a rarity since Jeremiah had known him. "I know what the Lord calls me to do, and when I am not sure, I read scripture and pay attention to what He is telling me to do. Everything you could possibly want to know is answered in the Bible."

Jeremiah stood and stretched his legs. "I need to get back home. I promised my dad I'd help him clear a section of the yard for some tomatoes and peppers."

"You can bring home anything you need from here," Abe offered. "We have plenty to share with the workers."

Shelley's feet ached from running all over the restaurant. Jocelyn had called in and said she'd be late—and she still hadn't shown up.

"Shelley!" The sound of Mr. Penner's voice booming across the restaurant startled her. He was generally fairly calm, but something seemed to be bothering him lately.

"Yes, Mr. Penner?"

"You know I like to keep the ketchup bottles filled." He wagged his finger toward the booths along the front window. "Those over there are half-empty."

"I'll do it right now," she said.

Shelley skittered around, filling ketchup bottles, checking sugar and saltshakers, and taking orders for the next half hour. When the door opened, she started toward the front until she realized it was Jocelyn.

"Hey there," Jocelyn said as though she didn't have a care in the world. "Been busy?"

"Ya," Shelley said, trying as hard as she could to keep the annoyance from her voice. "Are you here to work or talk?"

Jocelyn made a face. "Don't get all crazy stressed on me. Give me a chance to put on my apron."

Shelley took a deep breath and slowly let it out. Crazy stressed wasn't the phrase for what she was feeling. It was more like annoyance that someone wasn't doing her job and expected to be treated as though she were.

Jocelyn didn't waste any time getting ready to work. When she came around from behind the wall dividing the kitchen from the dining room, she was ready to take orders. Shelley made her way toward her and whispered an apology. "I should not have taken my frustration out on you."

"Hey, no problem. I can't say I wouldn't be taking your head off if you waltzed in two hours after your shift was supposed to start. So how's the special today?"

"It's good. Mrs. Penner made some extra coconut cream pie."

"Yum." Jocelyn gave a thumbs-up. "I'll let everyone know they need to save room for dessert."

Shelley had mixed feelings about Jocelyn. In spite of her odd hairstyle, clothes, and manner of speech, there seemed to be a sweetness hidden beneath a somewhat crusty exterior. Mr. Penner probably saw that, too, but Shelley doubted Mrs. Penner did, based on the glaring looks the older woman gave the newest employee.

After Shelley's customers had been served, she let them know she was leaving for the day and that Jocelyn would take care of them. The first few times she'd done that, she'd fully expected Jocelyn to keep her tips. But she'd been surprised each time when she came in the next day and spotted an envelope with her name on it. Inside she'd found a pile of dollar bills, some change, and a note letting her know these were the tips Jocelyn had collected from her tables. At least she was honest.

Some of the local Mennonite and Amish customers seemed disturbed by Jocelyn. Mr. Penner had pretty much shrugged off their comments until he realized he might lose a few customers. He would have eventually said something to Jocelyn, but his wife beat him to it. Shelley had to admit that Jocelyn had toned her style of dress and personality down quite a bit. She wanted to ask Jocelyn what Mrs. Penner had said, but she didn't want to be rude or nosy. One thing she did notice was that afterward Jocelyn appeared to have the utmost respect for the boss's wife.

Before Shelley left for the day, Mr. Penner handed her a package. "If you don't mind, I need to get this to my wife before I come home."

Shelley took the package and hesitated in order to give him a chance to tell her what was in it. But he didn't, so she nodded. "I'll go straight there."

With a grin, he nodded. "Good girl. Now get on out of here while you have a chance."

As Shelley reached the door, she waved to Jocelyn. "I owe you big time," Jocelyn said. "Thanks for covering my tables."

Shelley smiled but didn't say anything. On the way to the Penners', she noticed that the air hung heavy with moisture, even though it hadn't started raining yet. She glanced up at the sky toward the Gulf of Mexico. A narrow row of dark clouds rolled toward land, so she quickened her step so she wouldn't be caught in a downpour. By the time she reached the Penners' house, she'd been splattered with a few large raindrops.

Mrs. Penner yanked the door open before Shelley finished knocking. "Come inside, young lady, before you get drenched."

Shelley did as she was told. It had been a while since she'd been in the Penners' house, but nothing had changed—except the absence of Mary. "I don't want to impose," she said softly.

"That's ridiculous," Mrs. Penner said in her typical stern manner. "Come on into the kitchen. I'll fix you something to eat. We can talk while the rain blows over."

Shelley had no idea what they'd talk about, but she followed Mrs. Penner. The aroma of baked sugar, cinnamon, and yeast wafted through the tiny house. Her mouth watered. "I just made a fresh batch of cinnamon rolls for that truck driver who stops by when he's in the area. He called Joseph and said he'd be coming over before closing." She pulled a pan out of the oven, intensifying the smells in the kitchen. "Want one?" She glanced over her shoulder at Shelley. "I have to let them cool for a few minutes before I ice them, but you can wait, can't you?"

There was no way Shelley could resist once she saw the golden-brown rolls dripping in gooey syrup and dotted with nuts. "Yes, ma'am. I can wait for one of your cinnamon rolls."

Mrs. Penner laughed. "I thought so. You look like you haven't been eating much lately. Anything you care to talk about?"

Shelley slowly shook her head. "I've just been very busy lately."

"So I've heard. You need to be careful about how you stay busy and who you are busy with. Some people can take your focus off the Lord."

There was no doubt what Mrs. Penner was talking about. Shelley instantly felt defensive, but she knew better than to argue her case. The only way Mrs. Penner ever changed her mind about someone was to see that person in action.

Mrs. Penner set the rolls on a cooling rack then poured some coffee into two mugs, which she carried to the table. "Sugar and cream?"

"Yes, please."

After they both had their coffee fixed like they wanted, Mrs. Penner joined Shelley at the table. "Jeremiah has always been somewhat spirited, as my daughter once was. You know what happened to her."

Shelley looked Mrs. Penner in the eye and saw the wisdom borne of pain. "Yes, I know."

"Well? Aren't you going to tell me Jeremiah is different?" Mrs. Penner lifted an eyebrow as she waited for Shelley's answer.

"I would like to, but I'm not sure."

Mrs. Penner offered one of her rare smiles. "Smart girl. It's always a good idea to take a wait-and-see attitude before jumping into something. He's not keeping it a secret that he wants to court you. Our Mary has tried to convince us that Jeremiah is a changed man, and she reminds us that he helped Abe escort that evil monster who tried to hurt her out of the restaurant so the police could take him away." She sipped her coffee then set down her mug before looking back up at Shelley. "But it's easy to do one act of kindness in front of an audience. We need to see if he continues or if the temptations of his old life drive him away again."

"Yes, I agree."

"He needs to be consistent. I don't want you getting hurt by someone who isn't sincere."

Shelley looked at the older woman and nodded. "Even if Jeremiah is sincere, I have to help my mother with William."

Mrs. Penner leaned forward with a hint of a smile. "How is sweet William?"

"He's fine, but he's starting to show some independence, and my mother doesn't know what to do about it."

"Yes, I can see how that would be troublesome to her." Mrs. Penner stood and walked over to the counter to ice the cinnamon rolls.

"Would you like some help?"

"Gracious no," Mrs. Penner said with a chuckle. "You'd just get in the way."

Even though Shelley understood that Mrs. Penner spoke brusquely but was a good woman deep down, she was taken aback and silenced.

"Here," Mrs. Penner said as she placed a small plate

filled with a fluffy-looking roll covered in icing in front of Shelley. "Taste that, and let me know if you like it. It's a new recipe that I'll make in the restaurant if it turns out good enough."

There was never any doubt Shelley would like it. After all, it was common knowledge around Pinecraft that Mrs. Penner's cooking had put Penner's Restaurant on the map of almost every tourist who visited Sarasota.

The first words that came to mind when Shelley tasted the roll were totally yummo! She giggled at how much influence Jocelyn had over some of her thoughts.

Mrs. Penner spun around and scowled. "What is so funny?"

Shelley finished chewing and nodded her satisfaction. "This is delicious."

The scowl on the older woman's face faded to a hint of a grin. "That is what I like to hear." She turned back to finish icing the rest of the rolls when someone knocked on the door. "Go see who that is, Shelley. I'm not expecting anyone."

Shelley opened the door and took a step back. "Jeremiah…what are you doing here?"

"Who is that, Shelley?" Mrs. Penner called from the kitchen.

"It's Jeremiah," Shelley called back before turning back around to face Jeremiah.

"I stopped by the restaurant with some produce from the farm. Mr. Penner asked me here to offer you a ride home, since it's pouring out."

"Umm…" Shelley glanced over her shoulder then turned back to Jeremiah. "I can wait until it stops raining."

Jeremiah glanced over Shelley's shoulder. "Hello, Mrs. Penner."

Chapter Four

"Jeremiah, what are you doing here?"

Mrs. Penner's tone left no doubt that she didn't want him in her house. "I...uh, I came to see if Shelley needed a ride home since it's raining."

"She can wait until it stops."

Shelley cleared her throat, glanced at Mrs. Penner then turned around to face Jeremiah. His heart lurched at the quick connection he felt with Shelley. "I really should be getting home. My mother is expecting me."

Mrs. Penner tightened her lips and folded her arms. "She'll understand since it's raining."

Shelley gave her a look of apology. "Mother is having a difficult time lately, and she needs me."

Jeremiah felt bad for Mrs. Penner, despite her opinion of him. In fact, he couldn't really blame her after his past. "I promise I'll take her straight home," he said.

The woman blinked and abruptly turned as she mumbled something very softly. He could barely hear her, but he was pretty sure she said, "Promises are only as good as the person who makes them."

After walking Shelley to the passenger side of the car with the umbrella, Jeremiah ran around to the driver's side. "This rain came out of nowhere."

Shelley's eyes were focused on her hands folded in her lap. "I'm sorry about what Mrs. Penner said, but you have to understand. After what happened with Mary's mother…the Penners suffered quite a bit for many years."

"Oh, I do understand." He turned the ignition and smiled at Shelley before pulling away from the curb. "She has every reason not to trust me after all the stunts I pulled."

"Oh." Shelley folded her arms and stared forward. "So what are some of these…stunts you pulled?"

Jeremiah smiled. "I'm afraid to tell you too many details, or you'll never speak to me again."

"Why do you think that?" Shelley asked.

Jeremiah shrugged. "You're already mad at me for leaving the church. Besides, I'm asking forgiveness while moving forward. Dwelling on the past is very unhealthy."

"And dangerous," she added. They rode in silence for a few minutes before Shelley spoke up again. "Are you planning to give up your car?"

Jeremiah chuckled. "Abe is trying to talk me into it, but that's the only thing I think I'll miss. It's nice to not have to rely on others for transportation. I like being able to get in my car and go wherever I want."

Shelley looked at him quizzically. "Where all do you go?"

He thought for a moment before shaking his head. "Not many places. Mostly just to the farm and around Pinecraft." He paused before giving her a brief glance. "And picking up one of my favorite people, so she doesn't have to walk home in the rain."

"I appreciate the ride, Jeremiah, but I would have been fine."

"I'm sure you would have, but it's nice to be able to offer you a ride. Did you know that I had a sports car before I decided to come back to the church?"

"Yes," Shelley said. "I remember seeing your bright-orange car."

"Abe advised me to at least swap for something less flashy before talking to the church elders." He pulled up in front of Shelley's house. "Will you be in church tomorrow?"

"Yes, of course. I never miss church."

He let out a deep sigh. "I'll be there, too. Maybe we can talk afterward."

"Maybe."

"Look, Shelley, you don't have to worry about me embarrassing you."

"It's not that I'm embarrassed."

"No, but you know what I mean. I don't want to get people thinking anything you don't want."

Shelley frowned. "I'm not sure what to say to that."

He hesitantly touched her arm. She inhaled deeply, cleared her throat, and slowly let out her breath.

"I wish I'd behaved differently in the past," he said.

"Wishing away things about the past is such a waste of time."

"Yes, I realize that. But again, you know what I'm talking about. I think things would be different between us if I had been more faithful."

"Maybe, but you don't know that for sure."

"True." He nodded toward the house. "We're being watched again."

She looked at him and smiled before getting out of the car. "Thank you for the ride, Jeremiah."

He waved and drove away. After he was out of sight of her house, he pulled over and said a prayer that Shelley would eventually care about him as much as he did her. *But I know, Lord, that it will take some time to undo the damage I've done. Guide me, and keep me on the path to do Your will.*

The next day Shelley woke up before the sun came up. Since she was the first person up, she quietly got dressed and went outside to wait until time to make the coffee.

"Get up, William," Shelley said as she stood over her brother, who refused to get out of bed. "You have to get ready for church."

He sat up and glanced around with a dazed look in his eyes. "I had a bad dream."

"Oh, sweetie, I'm sorry." Shelley sat down on the edge of his bed. "Do you want to tell me about it?"

William rubbed his eyes and shook his head. "No, it's too scary."

Seeing him like this first thing in the morning reminded Shelley of when he was a tiny boy. Her heart ached for the limitations he had in life, but he didn't seem to mind. Most of the time William was very happy, and he loved the Lord.

Shelley patted him on the arm and stood. "Get up, and get ready. I'll have breakfast waiting for you." She got to the door when she heard him softly say her name. "Yes?"

"Is Mother feeling better?"

"I think so. Let's talk about that later, maybe after church."

Gray clouds hung over the Gulf of Mexico, and the humidity was high, but it hadn't started raining yet. Shelley and William led the way to church, with their parents directly behind them. She could hear her father's voice as he spoke softly to her mother.

They arrived in time to greet some of their friends. William and her father went to one side of the church, while Shelley and her mother joined the women on the other side. Her mother's silence disturbed Shelley, but she didn't know what to say. As they sat down, she lowered her head and prayed for her mother's moods to improve.

Shelley glanced up as Jeremiah entered the church. Her breath caught in her throat, and she had to fan herself. She looked in the opposite direction, hoping her mother wouldn't notice what had gotten her in such a state.

Throughout the church service, the very fact that she was in the same room as Jeremiah hung heavy in her mind. It bothered her to feel the way she did. After all, Jeremiah obviously wasn't the ideal match for her. Everyone close to her knew that, but her heart clearly wasn't getting the message.

After church they went outside, and William didn't waste any time joining Shelley and their mother. Jeremiah stood off to the side, occasionally glancing her way but not taking a step in her direction. She knew he was keeping his distance for her sake.

In spite of the fact that Shelley, William, and their mother stood by the sidewalk waiting to walk home, their father continued chatting with some of his friends. When Mary walked out of the church, she spotted Shelley and joined them.

"It's mighty humid today," Mary said. "I thought it would be pouring by now, but the storm seems stalled over the water."

William frowned. "I don't like to walk in the rain."

Shelley forced a laugh. "He hates getting his head wet."

"It makes my hair soggy."

Mary smiled. "I know that feeling."

"Where is Abe?" Shelley's mother said. "Shouldn't he be out of the church by now?"

"He's helping Jeremiah fix one of the baseboards that came loose."

Shelley's mother looked over at her husband and shook her head but didn't say anything else. An uncomfortable silence fell among them.

Finally, Abe walked outside. Mary extended her hand toward him, and he took it as he joined the women.

"It was wonderful seeing you this morning, Shelley," Mary said. "I miss talking to you every day at the restaurant."

"You have no business missing anything about your old life," Shelley's mother said. "You have a nice husband who gives you a good life."

Shelley wanted to find a rock and crawl under it, but Mary smiled at her and winked. "Maybe Abe and I can have you out to the house someday soon."

"Perhaps you can talk some sense into my daughter. She's been riding in the car with that Jeremiah boy lately. Her father and I don't like it one bit."

Mary gave Shelley's arm a squeeze. "I'll stop by the restaurant soon. We'll talk later."

After Mary left, Shelley's father joined them. "Let's go home, family. I'm starving." He gazed off into space as he did often. Once Shelley was old enough to help out more around the house, he'd found ways to be absent—both physically and mentally.

Since her mother hadn't bothered with meals lately, the task had fallen on Shelley. She was beginning to resent the fact that too much was expected of her, yet her mother found fault with everything she did.

"I like Mary," William said. "She's nice."

"And she has a good head on her shoulders, that girl," their mother said from behind. "She knew she couldn't do any better than Abe, so she latched on to him so he could take care of her."

Shelley couldn't hold back any longer. "Mother, I don't think she married Abe just because he could take care of her. Abe and Mary fell in love."

"Maybe so. But you need to start thinking about finding a man who can take care of you, and I'm not talking about Jeremiah. He left the church once, and you never know when he'll lose interest again and take off for who knows where."

Shelley glanced over her shoulder at her father, hoping for support, but he was clearly not listening. He'd dropped back a few steps, and he appeared to be deep in thought.

Since it seemed pointless to argue with her mother, Shelley decided to keep her mouth closed. William spotted a seagull as it headed toward the beach. "Remember when we were on that picnic, and a bird just like that one tried to steal our lunch?"

"Yes," Shelley said, grateful for the diversion. "Maybe if you hadn't fed him that potato chip, he wouldn't have known we had food."

"It wasn't my fault. I was trying to keep him away from the chicken."

"A bird eating chicken." Shelley shook her head. "That's just wrong."

"I like chicken," William said. "I bet the bird does, too."

"William! Chickens are birds." The scolding tone in their mother's voice startled both William and Shelley. "They shouldn't even want to eat one of their own."

William scrunched his forehead and pondered that for half a block. Finally, he seemed to get the concept. "That's gross."

Shelley laughed. "Yes, it is definitely gross."

"Why would a bird eat another bird?"

"Maybe they're not smart enough to know it's a bird," Shelley teased. "They have bird brains."

"I'm not stupid, Shelley," William said. "I know that birds have bird brains."

Shelley tilted her head back and laughed. Before he had a chance to get his feelings hurt, she threw her arms around him and gave him a big hug. "I love you, William. You are the sweetest person I know."

He hugged her back. "Nuh-uh. You are the sweetest person I know."

"You are," Shelley countered.

"No, you are." William giggled and covered his mouth with his hand. "Mother's going to get mad if we keep this up."

Shelley turned slightly and looked at her mother before turning back. "I don't think she's even paying attention to us." Before he had a chance to look around, she nudged him and pointed. "Hey, William, look at that bird with the red wings!" She had to keep him from seeing their mother, whose cheeks were stained with fresh tears.

William went into a long, detailed discussion about

the types of birds in Florida, including the fact that many of them had already left for the summer. Shelley was relieved when they arrived home.

"Wanna help me in the kitchen, William?"

He looked at their father, who seemed out of sorts. "If Father doesn't mind."

Their father shook his head before heading out the back door, while their mother retreated to her bedroom.

"Looks like it's you and me, baby brother," Shelley said as she pulled a skillet out of the cupboard.

"I am not a baby."

She grinned at him. "You'll always be my baby brother, even when you're old and gray."

William touched the top of his head. "I don't have gray hair yet. You'll get it before I do."

"Don't remind me. Would you mind handing me the butter?"

They worked together in the kitchen, with Shelley cooking while William handed her ingredients and utensils. Shelley was grateful that they got along so well. She and their older brother Paul used to have a good relationship, but when he left the church, everything had changed. Paul's wife, Tammy, was a sweet woman who would do whatever Paul wanted to do, so when he used her as an excuse for not coming back to the church, Shelley knew it was more about what Paul wanted than Tammy's lack of Mennonite upbringing. At least they went to church, although their parents didn't approve of where they attended.

After lunch was ready, Shelley sent William to let

their mother know. She opened the back door, stepped out onto the patio, and called for her father. He looked up from where he'd been sitting since they'd gotten home, a sadness in his eyes like she'd never seen before.

"I'll be there in a minute."

"Shelley," William said. "Mother said she's not hungry."

She pondered what to do before turning off the stove and oven. "Let me go talk to her. Why don't you go ahead and set the table?"

Shelley tiptoed to their mother's bedroom door and knocked.

There was no answer, so she slowly turned the knob and opened the door to the darkened room. She could see the silhouette of her mother sitting in a chair, back straight, head bowed.

"Mother?"

"What?" Her mother glanced up, but the room was too dark to tell if she'd been crying.

"Lunch is ready. Are you not feeling well?"

"I already told William I'm not hungry."

"You need to eat something," Shelley argued.

"Just have William bring me a plate of food when he's finished with his."

"I'd really like for the family to eat together," Shelley said. "It's Sunday, and I think it's good for all of us to be together on the Lord's day."

"We can't all be together. Paul is gone, and I'm worried you're going to run off and do something stupid."

"Mother, I'm not going to do anything stupid."

"Something is different about you lately, Shelley. I think it has something to do with Jeremiah. I keep thinking you'll decide not to come home one day, and then what?"

Shelley took a few steps closer to her mother. "Is that what's upsetting you?"

"What is happening to our family?"

"Mother, our family is fine. I'm not about to leave, and Paul lives close enough that he can be here within a few minutes if we need him."

Silence fell between them. Shelley had no idea what to say to her mother, but she didn't want to leave her alone.

"I always imagined all my children getting married some day and living nearby in Pinecraft, raising my grandchildren in the church. Now that it's not happening, I'm left to wonder what will become of the lot of us."

"When—if—I ever get married, I'll live close to you and Father. And if the Lord blesses me with children, they'll grow up in the church."

"And then there's William. Who will take care of him after your father and I are gone?"

Shelley closed the distance between herself and her mother. She reached down and took her mother's hand in hers. "You know that I will always make sure William has a home and all his needs are taken care of. The Lord doesn't want us to be anxious about the future, so please stop worrying."

"I know I'm not supposed to worry."

"We're not supposed to worry, but I think it's something we all do as humans."

"I suppose so."

Shelley took a chance and tugged at her mother, hoping she'd rise to join the rest of the family in the kitchen. She held her breath for a few seconds until her mother gave in and followed.

William had the table set, with all the food in serving bowls on the table. Their father stood at the head of the table, bent over his chair, appearing to be praying. He glanced up and looked at Shelley. "I'll say the blessing for our meal."

As he prayed, Shelley forced herself to focus on his words and not on her mother, who stood rigidly by her chair. Finally, her father sat down, waited for the rest of the family to sit, picked up a platter, put a small amount of chicken on his plate, and passed it to William.

Although Mother had been through short bouts of this bad mood throughout Shelley's life, she seemed to be getting worse. After dinner, Shelley found a way to whisper to her father and ask if they could talk. He looked at her a moment and then nodded.

"Shelley and I are going for a walk," her father said. "We'll be back shortly."

Mother gave them a quizzical look and then turned back around without saying a word. Shelley dreaded having to explain later.

Once they reached the edge of the block, Father slowed down. "What is on your mind, Shelley?"

"I'm worried about Mother. She seems to be getting worse lately."

"*Ya.* I agree." He shoved his hands into his pockets. "I never know what to say to her."

"I'd like to talk with the pastor about it."

"*Neh.* Not a good idea. Your mother would be very unhappy with that kind of attention."

"But she needs help," Shelley argued. "And we obviously can't do anything to fix whatever is wrong with her."

"We can continue to pray." He cleared his throat. "That is what I've been doing."

"So have I."

"While you're at it, pray that Paul will come back to the church. Your mother blames Tammy for his leaving, but he was always so strong-willed, I doubt Tammy has anything to do with it."

This was the most conversation Shelley could remember having with her father since becoming an adult. "*Ya*, I'll pray for Paul, Tammy, and the children. I would like to see Lucy and Grady more often."

"So would I." Father placed his hand on Shelley's back and gently turned her around. "We need to go back home, or your mother will worry." He smiled. "In her frame of mind, I don't want to give her anything else to worry about."

William met them at the door when they got back home. "I want dessert, and Mother says I have to wait for the rest of the family."

Father grinned. "Then let's have dessert."

"Who wants lemon cake?" Shelley asked as she made a beeline for the kitchen. "Mr. Penner sent me home with some on Friday, and I saved it for today."

"I like lemon cake," William said. "So does Mother."

"I'll have a small slice," their father said.

Shelley cut the cake into slices, including one for her mother, taking a chance that she'd have a little. She set them down in front of each family member and then carried hers to the table and sat down.

William devoured his, and her father ate his slowly. Her mother stared down at it but didn't lift her fork.

"This is very good, Mother. Mrs. Penner made several of them, and all the customers raved about it."

"I'm not hungry."

The sound of a chair crashing to the floor startled Shelley. She turned toward her father and saw that he was standing, glaring at her mother, the chair tipped over on the floor behind him. Even he looked surprised at his own outburst.

"Melba, the least you can do is take a bite. Can't you see how hard Shelley's trying to cheer you up?"

"Father—"

He held up a hand to shush her. "No, I need to say this. We love you, Melba, and it pains all of us to see you in this state. You need to feel the blessings of what you do have rather than mope around for what you think you don't have. Otherwise, you'll drive our daughter away, just like you—" He stopped himself, tightened his jaw, and glanced away, rubbing the back of his neck. "Please just stop dwelling on the negative. We have two beautiful grown children still living here."

The sound of Shelley's heart pounding equaled the impact of her father's outburst. "Mother, if you're not hungry…"

"I—I'll try to eat a little bit of cake," her mother whispered as she picked up her fork and stabbed at the golden yellow dessert in front of her.

Jeremiah drove Abe and Mary home. They'd invited him for Sunday lunch, which made him very happy. His parents had welcomed him back into their home, but he liked giving them some quiet time alone.

Mary made small talk from the backseat, but Jeremiah's mind was on Shelley and her family. Their sad expressions had touched his heart, and he wondered what was going on. He suspected it might have something to do with him, but he didn't want to be presumptuous and assume anything. After all, his mother had reminded him the world didn't revolve around him. The thought of that made him smile.

"You didn't hear a word I just said, did you?" Mary asked.

"Um…" Jeremiah glanced in his rearview mirror and caught her knowing gaze. "I'm sorry, Mary. My thoughts today are taking me somewhere else."

Mary nodded. "I thought so. Is it Shelley?"

Abe turned and looked at his wife over his shoulder. "Jeremiah might not want to share his private thoughts, Mary."

"No, that's okay. I need to be more transparent. One of the things I've learned is that I have to accept accountability to other believers." Jeremiah pondered how to form his thoughts into words before continuing. "Did you notice how sad Shelley's family seemed in church this morning?"

"Sometimes people get sad," Abe said. "I'm sure they have their reasons."

"Oh, Abe, it's not that simple," Mary said. "Yes, Jeremiah, I did notice. I think something might be wrong with Mrs. Burkholder."

"Do you think she's sick?" Jeremiah asked.

Mary shook her head, shrugged, and frowned. "I don't know. Perhaps I should talk to Shelley about it."

Abe turned around again. "That might not be such a good idea. If Shelley wants to discuss her family, she'll do it in her own time."

Jeremiah listened to his friends discuss what Mary should do. As they spoke, he became more convinced than ever that Shelley had some deep troubles that no one would ever know about unless someone who cared about her—someone she trusted—pried it out of her. And the only person he thought might be able to do that was Mary.

"No disrespect, Abe, but I think that it might help if Mary offered to pray for whatever is bothering Shelley."

Abe's expression was vague, but after a few seconds he slowly nodded. "If it is done in the correct way, it might be a good idea. Would you mind doing that, Mary?"

Again, Jeremiah looked at Mary's reflection in the mirror. She looked back at him and smiled. "I'll do what I can. Shelley has always been there for me."

Jeremiah turned onto the road leading to the Glick farm. A sense of peace washed over him as he realized how far he'd come from the life he'd transgressed to right after he got out of school. "This is a beautiful piece of property, Abe."

"I'm glad you like it. Would you ever consider having your own farm someday?"

"That would be nice, but property is very expensive these days. I'm not sure if or when I'll ever be able to afford to have my own place."

"Pray about it," Abe advised. "You might discover an opportunity that you never thought possible."

Mary let out a chuckle. "Come on, Abe, why don't you tell Jeremiah what we've been discussing?"

"Maybe later."

Jeremiah pulled to a stop in front of the old farmhouse, put the car in *Park*, and turned toward Abe. "What is Mary talking about?"

Mary got out of the car and waited for the men. They started walking toward the house when she turned to face them. "You two go talk while I get lunch on the table. It'll be about half an hour."

Abe grinned at his wife then turned to face Jeremiah. "My wife is a wise woman, and she doesn't believe in waiting for things."

Jeremiah ran his fingers through his hair. "Both of you are talking in riddles. Since you've decided to let me in on this one, let's talk now. I'm with Mary on not liking to wait."

Chapter Five

They walked past the barn toward a field that had obviously not been worked in years. Jeremiah looked out over the flat terrain before turning to face Abe, who shielded his eyes. "What do you think about all that land?"

"It looks good," Jeremiah replied. "Why? Are you thinking about planting some crops on it?"

"Been thinking about it."

"Any idea what you want to plant?"

Abe shook his head, removed his hand from his face, and looked Jeremiah directly in the eye. "It's all up to you."

"Me?" Now Abe was back to talking in riddles, and Jeremiah had no idea how to figure out this one.

"*Ya*, I'd like to sell it to you."

Jeremiah let out a nervous laugh. "If I had two spare nickels to rub together, I'd consider trying to find a way to buy it, but I can't afford to right now—at least not until my debt is paid off."

"This land has been sitting here for years. It's a shame to let it go to waste. Mary and I have been talking about a way for you to buy it, and she actually came up with a good idea. I'll put you to work on it and let you have one of the men who helped remove the barn to work for you. Whatever crops you plant will be yours, but the land will continue to be mine. As you turn a profit, you can pay me for working it. You should do well with the hundred acres I want to sell you."

"A hundred acres?"

Abe offered a clipped nod. "*Ya.* That's what we have here."

"I appreciate it, Abe, but that's way too generous."

Abe shrugged. "Not really. That land is just sitting there doing nothing. If you work it, once the harvest comes in I won't have to pay your salary since you'll be making money off the crops. You will also pay the man who helps you."

"But before the crops come in, I'll have to work another job."

"*Ya*, you'll continue to work for me. I'm sure I'll have plenty for you to do around here, but when you're finished for the day, you'll go over and tend your own crops." He gave Jeremiah a serious look. "You will have to work very long hours, but since you've been with me, I can tell you are able to do that."

Jeremiah looked back over the land, this time from a different perspective. All that land could be his if he said yes. It sure was a nice proposition.

"When do you want an answer?"

Abe gave him a puzzled look. "Why do you ask that?"

"I should probably consider it," Jeremiah said.

"What is there to consider? You want land, and I'm offering you a good deal on a hundred fertile acres that I can't use. You will be able to repay your debt much more quickly with your own crops."

Indeed. Jeremiah had become so conditioned to look for the other person's ulterior motive, he'd been afraid to give Abe a quick decision.

He pondered the pros and cons of taking Abe up on his offer. Mary hollered that lunch was ready, and Abe let her know they'd be right there.

Abe gestured toward the house. "Let's go eat. Mary always puts a lot of work into cooking, and I don't want to act like I don't appreciate her."

"Good move." Jeremiah fell into step beside Abe, and they walked in silence for about a hundred yards. Before they reached the house, Jeremiah had made up his mind. "I'll do it. I mean, if you are serious about wanting to do this deal for the land, I'd like to take you up on it."

Abe leveled him with a serious glare. "I am always serious about any offer I make." Then he relaxed.

"Yes, I know that, and I'm serious, too. This is probably the best opportunity I'll ever have, and it's definitely something I want to do."

"Good. I'm glad you want to have your own crops. I always thought it was such a waste not to do something with that land. Some commercial developers have offered me more money than I'd ever need in my lifetime, but I thought the land could be put to much better use than what they were proposing." He shook his head. "Converting farmland so close to my home could turn out to be a disaster."

"We'll be neighbors for life," Jeremiah pointed out.

"*Ya*, that is true."

If Jeremiah had ever doubted his decision to come back to the church he'd so abruptly left years ago, that was erased by Abe's simple statement. "Thank you, Abe. I'll do everything I can not to let you down."

"I'm not worried about that. I have faith that you'll find the right crop to work."

Jeremiah noticed the glance between Abe and Mary and then the twinkle in her eye when she realized he'd taken them up on their offer. A broad smile covered her lips as she gestured toward the table. "Jeremiah, why don't you say the blessing today?"

After the "amen," Mary handed Jeremiah the platter of sliced ham. He piled his plate with a couple of slices, a heaping spoon of scalloped potatoes, green beans, and fresh tomatoes. Abe spoke very little, except to tell Jeremiah some of the crops he'd considered for the property.

"But it's ultimately up to you," he added. "I don't want to interfere in your business decisions."

Jeremiah blotted his mouth with the cloth napkin and placed it back on his lap. "I like the idea of lemons, tomatoes, and peppers."

"We know those will do well. After you establish

your crops, you can experiment with different varieties and perhaps add new plants as you get comfortable," Abe said. He turned to Mary. "What is for dessert?"

"In honor of our celebration, I made two desserts—coconut cake and peanut butter pie from my grandmother's recipe."

"I would like some of both," Abe said. "How about you, Jeremiah?"

Still feeling as though he was floating from Abe's offer, he nodded as he patted his belly. "I might regret it later, but that sounds good. I'd hate to have to decide between those two options."

"Good!" Mary hopped up from the table to cut the pie and cake. She came back with dinner-size plates for the men, and then she went back to the counter to cut herself a small slice of pie.

"This is excellent, Mary," Jeremiah said after taking a bite of each dessert. "Your grandmother taught you well."

Mary blushed and lowered her head. Jeremiah glanced over at Abe, who smiled at his wife. The love between them was powerful and evident. Jeremiah sent up a silent prayer that he'd find a life partner who was as perfect for him as Abe and Mary were for each other. He wanted that person to be Shelley, but only if she was the one the Lord had picked out for him.

After they finished eating, Jeremiah watched Abe jump into action helping Mary. His own father had never lifted a finger around the house, but he could see the advantages of pitching in. Mary clearly appreciated Abe's help, and it gave them more opportunities to interact. Jeremiah filed that in his memory bank for future use. Then he helped as much as he knew how to.

After everything was put away, Mary said she was tired and needed to lie down for a little while. Abe asked him to join him for a walk.

Once he and Abe were far enough away from the house that Jeremiah didn't have to worry about Mary hearing them, he asked, "Is Mary okay? I don't remember her getting tired in the middle of the day before."

Abe chuckled. "*Ya*, she's doing just fine for a woman who is going to have a baby in about six months."

Jeremiah's eyebrows shot up. "She is? You and Mary are going to be parents soon?" His heart pounded as hard as it would have if he'd been the father. "That's great! I'm happy for you!"

"We are happy, too."

"Have you told Mary's grandparents yet?"

"*Neh*, so if you don't mind, I'd like for you to keep that bit of information to yourself. We've been asking them to come out to see us, but her grandfather hasn't been able to get away from the restaurant since they hired that new girl, and the late-shift manager is on vacation." Abe chuckled. "He's worried that some of the people will hurt Jocelyn's feelings about the way she looks and acts."

"Jocelyn is okay," Jeremiah said. "And I think she can handle anything people say to her."

"That is what Mary told him, but he isn't ready to leave her alone yet."

"So you and Mary will have to go to town to tell them the news," Jeremiah said.

"Ya. We are going there on Wednesday."

Jeremiah looked over toward the land that would soon be his, stretched his arms out, and sucked in a deep breath. This was turning out to be a wonderful day—full of delicious food and the best news he'd heard in ages.

Although Jeremiah could have hung around all day staring at the property, he didn't want to overstay his welcome, so he thanked Abe, asked him to let Mary know how much he appreciated all the fabulous food, and headed back to his parents' house in town. As he drove, he thought about having his own land and even building a house to live in with his future wife and children. The image brought a smile to his face like nothing else ever could have—not even his hot-orange sports car that he'd had such a hard time giving up.

Mr. Penner had asked Shelley to stick around later on Wednesday, so he could visit with Mary and Abe when they stopped by his house. The woman who worked as the late-shift manager was visiting family in Ohio, and he didn't want to leave Jocelyn in charge yet.

"Mind if I eat first before we get slammed?" Jocelyn asked.

"Sure, that's fine. I'm not all that hungry anyway." Shelley hadn't seen Jeremiah in several days. She knew he'd gone over to the Glick farm and had lunch with Abe and Mary on Sunday, so she'd planned to chat with

Mary about it. But Mary hadn't come by the restaurant lately, which Shelley thought was odd.

Jocelyn leaned over and waved her hand in front of Shelley's face. "You okay?"

Shelley startled. "Um...*ya*, I'm just fine."

"You seem out of sorts lately. Anything you wanna talk about?"

"*Neh*. I have a lot on my mind lately."

"I can imagine." Jocelyn started walking toward the kitchen to get her meal. She stopped and turned back to Shelley. "If you ever want to unload, I'm a good listener."

"Thanks, Jocelyn."

Shelley doubted Jocelyn would ever understand anything about her life—from being Mennonite to having a mother who was falling deeper into depression and a brother who'd never be completely independent. Sometimes her life felt weighty and more than she could bear until she prayed and allowed the Lord to remind her through scripture that there was more to life than what she had on earth.

The dining room was slow, which allowed both Jocelyn and Shelley to eat a little something before the crowd arrived. Shelley had just served the customers in the corner booth when she glanced up and saw Jeremiah walking toward her. She tried to be nonchalant when she greeted him, but the instant she opened her mouth, merely a squeak came out.

"Mind if I sit over there?" he asked, pointing to one of the empty tables in the dining room.

"That is fine," Shelley replied, her voice softer than usual. "I'll be right with you as soon as I bring these orders back to the kitchen."

As soon as she got out of Jeremiah's line of vision, Shelley stopped, took a deep breath, and tried to regain her composure. After not seeing him for a while, she'd managed to put him out of her mind—at least, she thought she had.

"Want me to take over?" Jocelyn said as she breezed by.

"Whatever for?"

Jocelyn offered an understanding grin. "Atta girl. Keep that attitude, and you'll be able to fool him into thinking you don't care. Guys like girls who play hard to get."

"I'm not—" Shelley stopped herself to keep from defending herself, which would make it seem as though she was playing a game with Jeremiah. Well, she wasn't, was she? She paused for a moment to think about it. No, she definitely wasn't playing any sort of game. She pushed that thought from her mind and plowed ahead.

After she felt that she could hold a decent conversation with Jeremiah, Shelley went back out to take his order. He asked for a piece of pie and some milk.

"Is that all?" she asked.

"Yes, I had dinner. I just wanted to stop by and see you."

Shelley allowed a smile to tweak her lips. "You don't have to order dessert if you're not hungry."

"I can always make room for some of Mrs. Penner's delicious pie."

"Okay, I'll bring it right out." Shelley turned and started toward the kitchen when she heard the jingle at the door. She turned around and saw Mr. and Mrs. Penner walking in, followed by Abe and Mary—all of them wearing broader grins than she'd ever seen on any of them. She glanced over her shoulder and spotted Jeremiah with the same expression. They were all definitely on to something, and she felt left out.

As Shelley placed a slice of pie on the plate and poured Jeremiah a glass of milk, she mentally lectured herself to act normal. She squared her shoulders and headed out with Jeremiah's order in both hands.

He was still grinning as she approached his table. Mary, Abe, and the Penners stood on the other side of the restaurant chatting with one of the customers.

"Here you go, Jeremiah. Will there be anything else?"

Jeremiah shook his head and gestured toward the other side of the booth. "Join me?"

Shelley blinked. "I can't do that. I'm working."

"You don't look too busy to me."

She was about to argue with him, but Mr. Penner's voice stopped her. "Go ahead and sit down, Shelley. You've worked hard all day. You've earned it."

Not one to argue with the boss, Shelley sat down across from Jeremiah, awkwardly fidgeting with the edges of her apron. She glanced at him but quickly looked down at the table.

"I wanted to share the good news with you," Jeremiah said. Shelley braced herself. Often other people's good news was her bad news, like when Peter had told her he was engaged to another woman, so it could have been anything, including courting someone else. The notion of that bothered her more than she wanted it to.

"Do you want to hear it or not?" he asked, his smile fading as a look of concern covered his face.

She looked up at him and nodded. "Yes, of course I'd like to hear your good news, Jeremiah. Why wouldn't I?"

"I don't know. You acted sort of strange there for a moment." He put down his fork, rubbed his hands together, cast a brief glance over toward the Penners, and then faced her again. "I am about to be a landowner."

"A landowner?"

He nodded. "Abe and I have worked out a deal for me to purchase some of the land he isn't farming. I'll continue to work for him until we get everything in place."

"That's nice. I mean, you'll be able to grow crops, right?"

"Yes, and I'll continue to work closely with Abe."

"I'm very happy for you."

Shelley started to stand, but Jeremiah placed his hand on her wrist and tilted his head toward the table. "Please stay. I'm happy, and I want to tell you all about it."

Since Mr. Penner had ordered her to sit down, she decided to remain and listen to Jeremiah's chatter about what he wanted to do with the farmland. She couldn't help but get caught up in his excitement.

"I'll start out with more citrus, and since Abe has oranges and grapefruit, I'm planting lemon and lime trees. It'll take a few years before they produce enough, so I'll add tomatoes, peppers, and whatever else I can get to grow."

"Do you know how to do all that?" Shelley asked. "After all, you haven't been working on the farm all that long."

"I know the basics, and I'm still learning. But like I said, I'll work closely with Abe. He told me about a county extension course that I can take to learn some of the science of farming."

Jeremiah had come a long way in a very short time. Shelley hoped he was as sincere as he sounded.

"And as soon as I can, I plan to start building a house on the land."

She was uncomfortable as she felt his gaze lingering on her. "A house is nice."

"I want a house big enough for a family."

Shelley's heart twitched. "Yes, of course."

"Shelley? Look at me."

She slowly widened her eyes to look directly at Jeremiah, but she didn't know what to say. He didn't speak either. Their gazes locked for several seconds before Mr. Penner joined them.

"So, Shelley," the older man said. "What do you think about Jeremiah having his own farm?"

She welcomed the diversion. "I think it's wonderful. He'll be a very good farmer—I'm sure."

Mr. Penner chuckled. "I obviously interrupted at the wrong time. I'll leave now."

Shelley jumped up from the table. "Oh no. I need to go help prepare the dining room for tomorrow."

Mr. Penner glanced over his shoulder. "*Ya*, that's a good idea." He leaned toward Shelley and lowered his voice. "Jocelyn is still a bit slow, but she seems to be working out just fine. Now that you've worked with her for a while, how do you like her?"

Shelley considered how friendly Jocelyn had been with her and how much the customers seemed to like her. "I like her."

"Good. She's not much past twenty, and she still has a lot to learn." Mr. Penner straightened up and tugged at his suspenders. "My decision to hire her wasn't a bad one like some people thought it might be."

As Shelley took off toward the kitchen to get a couple of rags and cleaner for the tables, she heard Mr. Penner and Jeremiah exchange a few more comments. When she heard the jingle at the front door, she thought they'd all left. However, she came back out and spotted Jeremiah still sitting at the booth.

"I thought you left," she said as she wiped his table clean.

"No, I'm sticking around to take you home after you close the restaurant."

"You don't need to do that," she argued. "I can walk home."

"I know I don't need to do that, but I want to. It's important to me."

Shelley accepted the fact that Jeremiah wouldn't take no for an answer, so she finished cleaning up as quickly as she could. Jocelyn had gotten better about knowing what to do, so Shelley didn't have to give her as much instruction.

She removed her apron, placed all the rags and towels in the laundry bin, and walked out to the dining room. Jeremiah wasn't there.

"Looks like you got ditched," Jocelyn said.

"That's fine. I like walking home. It gives me time to think."

Jocelyn leaned back, narrowed her eyes, and shook her head. "If I didn't know you, I'd think you were lying through your teeth."

"Lying through my teeth?"

"Yeah, that's like lying, only worse."

Shelley couldn't imagine a lie worse than a regular lie, and she didn't see how doing it through her teeth would change it. "I am not lying."

"I know you're not. You're the real deal." Jocelyn winked and playfully laughed. "I need to get outside since my car is in the shop. My ride will be here any minute."

"Would you like me to wait with you?" Shelley asked.

"No, you go on ahead. I'll be just fine."

The second they stepped outside, Shelley spotted Jeremiah standing over by his car talking to one of his old friends. She felt awkward and shy, and she wasn't about to go up to him while he was with that stranger.

She hesitated for a split second and then stepped down off the curb, being careful not to turn around and look at Jeremiah. She'd gone about ten feet when she heard Jeremiah call out to her. She stopped and turned around.

"Hey, Shelley, hold on a sec. Remember? I'm taking you home."

"I can walk."

"No, I'm taking you home." He said something to his friend that she couldn't hear and then jogged over to her. "That's one of the nicest guys I've ever met. In fact, he's the one who advised me to return to my roots."

"I thought you did that of your own accord."

"I did." Jeremiah waved to the man. "But Kyle was the first person I told I wasn't happy in that lifestyle."

"Did he take offense?"

"No, I don't think so. He said he thought people would accept me if they were sure I was sincere."

He opened the passenger door, and she got in. Shelley stared after Jeremiah's friend until he took off in his truck.

After Jeremiah got into the driver's seat, Shelley asked, "What was your friend Kyle doing over here in Pinecraft?"

"He was making a delivery to one of the businesses."

As they waited at a traffic light, Shelley decided to get Jeremiah talking about the farm, since that seemed to make him so happy. "When will you actually have your own land?"

"Abe is working something up, so we can eventually move the property to my name. Even before that, I'll work it like it belongs to me. Once I have it paid off from the money I get from the crops, it will be all mine." He cleared his throat. "Well, mine and my family's."

"How will you do that while still working for Abe?"

Jeremiah rubbed the back of his neck. "It'll be a lot of hard work, but like Abe said, I can do it this way, wait until I have enough money saved, or never have my own land."

"What made Abe think you'd even want to do this?"

"We used to talk about it when we were kids. Even though he's a year younger, I always looked up to him because he was the smartest and most focused kid I ever knew."

"I guess I never really paid that much attention to Abe," Shelley said. "I was too busy at home."

Jeremiah squinted as he pointed toward Shelley's house.

"Isn't that your brother out on the front lawn?"

Shelley turned and looked. "Yes, it's William. What is he doing?"

"I can't tell. He has his face on his knees. Looks like he might be sick or something."

As soon as Jeremiah pulled up in front of Shelley's house and stopped the car, Shelley hopped out and ran over to her brother. Jeremiah remained in the car for a couple of minutes, but William wasn't budging. He turned off the engine, got out of the car, and walked over toward Shelley and William.

"Need any help?"

Shelley was confused. "He's sobbing, but he won't tell me what's wrong."

"Let me see what I can do." Jeremiah drew closer and squatted down beside William. "Hey, buddy, what's the matter?"

William's sobbing grew softer, but he still didn't look up. Shelley felt helpless and had no idea what she should do.

Jeremiah pointed toward the house. "Maybe you can go inside and see if something is going on in there."

"I don't want to leave William alone."

"You're not," Jeremiah reminded her. "I'm right here. I won't leave until I know everything is okay."

Shelley went through the motions of walking into the house, calling out her mother's name, and getting no answer. This had happened before, but in the past William had been either in his room or out in the back-yard.

Her parents' bedroom door was closed, so she knocked. There was no answer. She slowly opened the door and saw the outline of her mother under the blanket on the bed.

"Mother, are you not feeling well?"

Her mother made a muffled sound and moved a leg. Shelley walked a little closer until she could touch her mother.

"What's going on, Mother?"

Her mother moaned and then threw the blanket away from her face. "Go away. I'm not feeling well."

"Have you spoken to William?"

"*Neh.* He opened the door, but I told him I needed to rest."

"Where's Father?"

"He hasn't come home from work yet." Her mother pulled the blanket back over her head. "Why don't you cook something for you and William?"

"All right." Shelley tiptoed out of the bedroom and went back out to the front yard. Her mother had seemed sad for years, but lately she'd gotten worse, and nothing Shelley did helped.

When she joined Jeremiah and William outside, they were sitting on the grass talking. Jeremiah glanced up and motioned her over. "William was just telling me that your mother is very sick. He's afraid she's going to die like your grandmother did when she wasn't able to get out of bed."

Shelley looked at Jeremiah but couldn't think of anything to say. She just stood there, silently making eye contact with him for what seemed like eternity until Jeremiah got up, brushed off the back of his trousers, and pulled William to his feet.

"Come on, buddy," Jeremiah said. "Let's go inside and help Shelley cook you some supper."

Chapter Six

Jeremiah saw that Shelley was just going through the motions of cooking, so he did everything he could think of to engage William in the process. William's sweet nature and innate desire to please others made the task not so difficult.

Once they had everything in the oven and cooking on the stovetop, Shelley went back to check on her mother. That left Jeremiah in the kitchen alone with William.

"Is Mother going to die?" William asked.

Not sure what was wrong with Mrs. Burkholder, Jeremiah hesitated before answering. He finally spoke some carefully chosen words. "Only the Lord knows the answer to that, William, but I don't think so. I just think something is making your mother very sad."

"But she can't get out of bed. When my grandmother was like that, she died."

"Do you ever feel sad?" Jeremiah asked.

William scrunched his face as he thought about it and then nodded. "*Ya*, sometimes."

"When you feel sad do you ever feel like being alone?"

"One time I did." William paused before continuing. "I remember when my big brother, Paul, moved out and stopped coming to see me. That made me very sad, and I wanted to sleep all the time."

"I think that's how your mother feels right now— like sleeping all the time because she's sad."

"Oh." William folded his arms, leaned against the cabinet, and frowned. "Is she still sad about Paul?"

"I don't know, but that could be part of it. As people get older and their children grow up, things change. Some parents don't know how to react to those changes."

William puffed out his chest. "I'm growing up."

Jeremiah smiled at him. "Yes, you are, and although your parents are proud of you, I'm sure they're sad they don't have a little boy anymore."

A look of understanding replaced William's worried expression. "Now I get it. Mother feels like she doesn't have a child to take care of."

Before Jeremiah could say anything, Shelley reappeared. "I think Mother is doing better. She asked me to bring something to eat when it's ready."

Jeremiah pulled her to the side as William stirred the contents of one of the pots. "Where is your father?"

"He's been working evenings lately. The store is

having to stay open later, and they rotate who works the late shift every six weeks."

"I think that might be part of the problem," Jeremiah said. "Not only is her youngest child about to be an adult who still needs help, but also her evening routine has been drastically changed." He glanced up at the stove. "Look at how well your brother is doing. He's such a kind person, and he doesn't mind pitching in when he knows what is needed."

Jeremiah's thoughtfulness tugged at Shelley's heart. His past transgressions still lingered in her mind, but his current actions pushed them further back.

"I'm starving," William said. "I think supper is ready."

"Then let's eat," Jeremiah said.

Shelley cast a teasing glance his way. "I thought you already ate."

"I've worked up an appetite." He handed her a serving spoon. "For scooping the beans," he explained.

Shelley laughed, planted her hands on her hips, and gave them a playful stern expression. "Who is in charge here?"

Jeremiah lifted his hands in surrender. "You definitely are."

Once again she laughed. "Good answer."

"I would never take that away from you."

William had the plates out of the cupboard and on the table. He headed back to the drawer and pulled out some flatware while Shelley handed Jeremiah some serving bowls for the food. The scenario felt right to Shelley—almost as though God had set them up as a small family. Her gaze met Jeremiah's, and she shuddered because she thought he might be feeling it, too.

"Here is a plate for Mother," William said. "Do you think I should cut her meat for her?"

Shelley was about to say no, that she'd do it, but Jeremiah spoke up. "That would be very nice, William. Thank you." He turned to Shelley and grinned.

After the food was ready for Mother, Shelley carried it to the bedroom, where her mother sat up in bed. Shelley pulled the blinds open to let in some of the early-evening light without making it too bright in the room.

"Do you want iced tea or lemonade?" Shelley asked.

"Some buttermilk would be good."

That was odd. Her father always drank buttermilk, but her mother rarely did. "Okay, I'll go get it. Do you need anything else while I'm in the kitchen?"

To Shelley's surprise, her mother smiled back at her. "No, thank you. This looks and smells very good."

After she delivered the buttermilk to her mother, she joined the men in the kitchen. "Will you please say the blessing, Jeremiah?"

Jeremiah's forehead crinkled. "I already asked William to, if you don't mind."

"Of course I don't mind." Shelley was pleased that Jeremiah had taken that step of action. Her parents had never asked William to say the family blessing, which she suspected was because he was the youngest person in the family. Jeremiah was giving William more responsibility, and she could tell that made William happy.

After the very sweet, short but heartfelt prayer, they passed the food around the table. William took larger portions than usual, but he was obviously hungry since they were eating an hour later than normal.

"The food was delicious, Shelley."

Shelley's attention shot up to the voice behind her. When she turned around, she saw her mother standing there, half-smiling, holding an empty plate.

"Mother, are you feeling better?"

Her mother closed her eyes and nodded. "Much better, now that I know my family cares enough about me to bring me food."

Shelley was surprised that her mother spoke so freely in front of Jeremiah.

"Mrs. Burkholder, why don't you join us?" Jeremiah said.

Shelley's mother blinked as though having to refocus. Her smile faded for a few seconds, but she managed to recover. "I am not so sure that's a good idea."

"Please," William begged. "It's just not the same when you and Father aren't here."

Shelley held her breath as her mother looked first at William then at Jeremiah. When her gaze settled on Shelley, she finally nodded. "I suppose I could join you for dessert." She sat down. "There is dessert, isn't there?"

"There's always dessert," Shelley said as she stood to get the banana cream pie out of the refrigerator.

"Just a small piece for me, please," her mother said.

"I want a big piece," William added.

Jeremiah lifted a hand. "Make that a big piece for me, too, and I'll do the dishes."

"All that hard work must be giving you an appetite," Shelley said as she sliced the pie and placed the servings on the dessert dishes. "Why don't you tell Mother about your plans?"

Jeremiah lowered his head and appeared bashful, something Shelley hadn't expected. She wondered if she'd messed up by talking about something he didn't want to discuss with anyone else yet. She was about to apologize when he started talking.

"I've been working on Abe's farm for the past few months. He knows I don't have enough money to buy my own farm yet, but it's something I've decided I want to do. So he offered to sell me a piece of his land that he hasn't been farming."

"If you don't have the money, how can you buy Abe's land?" her mother asked.

"Mother…" Shelley said, wishing she hadn't brought it up.

"That's okay, Shelley. I don't mind telling her," Jeremiah said as he lifted his hand in acceptance. "That's an excellent question." He turned back to her mother. "Abe is allowing me to go ahead and plant some crops after I finish working for him. When the crops are ready to harvest and sell, I'll pay him back with the profits."

"That's all good, Jeremiah, but after your past decisions, I'm surprised Abe has that much confidence in you. I certainly don't."

Once again, Shelley held her breath. She dared a brief glimpse in Jeremiah's direction, but he didn't look upset. He tightened his lips but nodded. "I understand why you feel that way. I've made more than my share of mistakes, so I fully expect to be scrutinized."

"At least you know that."

"Oh, I do. And I won't let Abe down. He has been very good to me."

Shelley carried William's and Jeremiah's pie to them first and then went back to get hers and her mother's. As they ate their pie, William told their mother all about how he'd helped cook supper.

Three weeks later, Jeremiah stood in front of the land he'd plowed with the help of Jonathan Polk's son, Charles, who was right next to him. They both remained silent for several minutes. The clearing and plowing had been much more difficult than Jeremiah had expected, but now that it was done, he felt better than he had in years. He'd accomplished something without anyone standing over him. In fact, he'd been the one giving direction to a very kind person who asked quite a few questions about the Mennonite church.

Jeremiah was pleased to have someone coming to him for answers, since he was often the one asking the questions. Charles said he liked the simple life of the Mennonite people, and he was considering adopting it.

Jeremiah said that was a decision only he could make, and he needed to pray about it. Charles said he had.

The land was mostly flat with a few very small hills and some trees in a cluster near where Jeremiah thought would be a good place to build a house. He envisioned a family home with a grassy front yard and a backyard where the children would run around, chase each other, and play ball.

Charles broke the silence. "Not bad for a couple of guys and some borrowed equipment, huh?"

"We got a lot done, with the Lord's help," Jeremiah said.

"Yes, we did." Charles turned to him and smiled. "And it feels mighty good."

"Thank you for helping me."

Silence fell between them once again. Jeremiah knew Charles had a huge decision ahead of him, so he gave his friend a chance to think without interruption.

"Do you think I'll be accepted since I wasn't raised in the church?"

Jeremiah nodded. "After what I did and being welcomed back, I think there's a very good chance…that is, if you're sincere. How do your parents feel about it?"

Charles sighed. "My dad is totally okay with it. In fact, if it weren't for my mom, I suspect he'd want to do it, too."

"Your mother doesn't approve?"

"It's not that she doesn't approve. She just isn't willing to make the change herself, so my dad can't very well do it alone."

"At least you have your family's support," Jeremiah said. "And it's something you need to pray about."

"I'd appreciate it if you'd pray for me, too," Charles said. "It's a huge decision that keeps me awake at night."

"The Lord doesn't want you to stay up all night worrying."

Charles placed his hand on Jeremiah's shoulder and bowed his head. Jeremiah had no doubt his friend was sincere.

"What's got you all tight-jawed and moody?" Jocelyn asked as they cleared away a large table together.

"All what?" Half the time Jocelyn said things that made no sense to Shelley.

One corner of Jocelyn's lip slanted upward in a half grin. "Sorry. Why are you so quiet? Did I say something that bugged you?"

Shelley shook herself. "No. I've just had a lot on my mind lately."

"Is your mom feeling any better? I overheard someone saying she's been sick."

"She seems to be doing a little better, now that my father has switched back to an earlier shift at work. She likes it when we're all home at night."

Jocelyn made a snorting sound. "I wouldn't know what that was like. My parents split before I could walk."

"That must have been awful," Shelley said.

"Not really. I didn't know any better since I don't remember a time when they were together."

Shelley wasn't sure what to say to that, so she finished wiping her side of the table without talking. Jocelyn was on the other side watching her.

"You confuse me," Jocelyn said.

"I do? What do you find confusing?"

"Everything. You never lose your temper, but I know you get upset. When I mess up, you never let me have it. When I first met you, I thought you didn't know any better, but now I know how smart and aware you are. You could level me out if you really wanted to."

Shelley shrugged. "What would be the point?"

"I don't know. But most people would tell me off or at least get mad. Do you ever get angry?"

"Of course I do," Shelley replied. "I'm human."

"Well, that's a relief."

Shelley glanced up in surprise and noticed the teasing expression on Jocelyn's face. She smiled back at her coworker. "You're funny."

Jocelyn giggled. "I'm glad you think so. Let's get this place cleaned up so you can get outta here."

Shelley appreciated Jocelyn's understanding and respect for her time. After she filled the last of the salt-shakers, she hung up her apron, said good-bye to the other people in the restaurant, and took off for home.

She stepped off the curb, half expecting Jeremiah to pull up and offer her a ride, but he didn't. He hadn't done that in several weeks. The only times she'd seen him were when he came into the restaurant when he was picking up something in town to take back to the farm and after church on Sundays. But even then, he was only civil toward her and offered her a few brief comments.

"I should be glad about that," she mumbled to herself as she strode home. Jeremiah had intruded on her heart, and with all the worries at home, she didn't need something else to think about. She was better off without the feelings he evoked when he was around.

By the time Shelley arrived home, she'd talked herself into thinking she was happiest without the complications of having Jeremiah in her life and acting like he was in love with her. Love? Where had that word come from?

"Shelley, is that you?" Her mother's voice pulled her from her thoughts.

"Yes, Mother. I'll be right there. Let me put my bag and shoes away first."

Shelley went to her room, hung her tote on the peg, took off her shoes, and put on some sandals as she mentally unwound from her day. Then she joined Mother in the kitchen.

"What can I do to help you?"

She was greeted with a smile. "Nothing. Have a seat, and I'll join you. Want some tea?"

Shelley slowly nodded. "*Ya*, that would be very nice. Want me to fix it?"

"*Neh*, I have the tea in the pot, and I'm just waiting for the water to boil." She carried a couple of cups to the table and set one in front of Shelley and placed one where she normally sat.

Shelley watched her mother move around the kitchen, light on her feet, as though she didn't have a care—completely opposite from her behavior a month ago. Several things had helped, including her father's shift change, William's increased doting, and being nurtured by a small group of women from the church. They'd heard about her depression, so they'd made it their mission to check on her daily.

A few minutes later, Shelley and her mother sat adjacent to each other at the kitchen table, blowing on their tea in silence. It felt nice knowing that things were going well—at least for now.

"How was your day?" her mother finally asked.

"It was good. Normal. Nothing happened."

Her mother smiled and lifted her cup to her lips, taking a sip. "Sounds peaceful."

"How about you? Did you have a good day?"

"*Ya.* The women from church checked on me this morning, but they didn't stay long." Mother's smile faded, and she sighed.

Shelley touched her mother's arm. "Is something wrong?"

"I'm not sure. I'm grateful to have your father home nights, and William seems happy. Paul has been stopping by whenever he gets a chance, and he's even offering to bring the children by more often." Her mother licked her lips and slowly raised her gaze. "The only thing I have left to worry about is you, Shelley."

"Me? Why are you worried about me?"

"I'm concerned about you and Jeremiah."

Shelley leaned back and shook her head. "I haven't seen much of Jeremiah lately. He's been working very hard on the land he's getting from Abe, so he doesn't have much time for anything else."

"I've heard he's doing that so he can take a wife and have a family."

"Maybe," Shelley said slowly. "But that's not my concern."

Her mother tilted her head, raised her eyebrows, and fixed her focus on Shelley. "Are you sure it is not your concern?"

"Why would it be?"

"According to one of the women from church, Jeremiah has his sights set on making you his wife."

"Something so serious requires more than Jeremiah's sights." Shelley tried to keep a light tone to her voice, but the impact of her mother's words and concern hit her hard. "And I haven't given it a thought."

"I wondered about that. Sometimes you can be so secretive I don't know what you're thinking or even doing."

"I would never do anything wrong, Mother. I thought you knew that about me."

"You are a good girl, Shelley, but I know what it's like to be a young woman. It might have been a long time ago, but sometimes the years between then and now seem so short."

"You and Father have been together a long time," Shelley observed.

"*Ya*, we have." An uncommon look of contentment softened her mother's features.

Shelley had never had a discussion about her parents' relationship with her mother, but now seemed like a good time to start. "Were you always in love with Father, or did you ever doubt your feelings for him?"

"Never… Well, maybe when we were very young, and he teased me unmercifully—I thought he was a pest. But after we became adults, he made his intentions very obvious, and I was smitten."

That sounded similar to how Jeremiah had been with Shelley, with the exception of when Jeremiah abandoned his faith. "Father was a pest?"

Her mother laughed out loud. "That is an understatement. He found ways to annoy me when we were in our early teens." She pursed her lips and blushed.

"I'd love to hear about this."

"For starters, he hid things and then asked me if I'd seen them. Once when we had a very big homework assignment, our teacher told us to put it on our desk before we went to lunch. When we came back, mine was gone. I panicked, but one look at your father let me know he was guilty."

"I remember Jeremiah doing something like that to me," Shelley blurted before thinking. The look on her mother's face made her shrink back. "But I'm sure it was different."

"Another thing your father did was jump out from behind things and frighten me."

Shelley had never seen that playful, mischievous side of her father. All she'd ever known was the stern, serious man who came home every night for supper and ate in near silence.

"But when we became old enough to consider courting, he let me know he'd acted out because he didn't know what else to do about his feelings for me." Shelley's mother smiled shyly. "And I admitted that I was flattered. After that, we knew we would eventually get married." She paused and looked Shelley in the eye. "There was never any doubt that we both loved the Lord because neither of us ever walked away and left our faith behind."

She got up and carried the teapot to the counter by the sink, ending the conversation. Shelley brought the two teacups and offered to do the dishes.

"I'll take care of this, Shelley. You've worked so hard lately. Why don't you go to your room and rest for a few minutes?"

As Shelley left the kitchen, she thought about her discussion with her mother. This had been one of the longest they'd had in a while, and she was grateful for the time. But it obviously was done for a purpose. A warning. Mother's final comment about never leaving faith behind had been directed at Jeremiah.

She closed her bedroom door, kicked off her shoes, and lay down on the lightweight summer quilt her grandmother had made. As she stared up at the ceiling, her conversation with her mother played through her mind.

Shelley knew that her parents had married young—much younger than she was now at the age of twenty-five. Most of the Mennonite couples she knew did. Their children often waited a little longer, though, so Shelley wasn't alone. The big difference between Shelley and some of the other single people her age was that she would have the responsibility of taking care of William for the rest of his life after her parents could no longer care for him, while the others could go into a marriage alone.

Jeremiah was the only man Shelley's age who actively engaged William in conversation. William clearly liked Jeremiah, but Shelley could tell when he'd heard something negative from their parents because he would always add a disparaging comment after anything positive he'd said about Jeremiah.

After a half hour of rest, Shelley got up, repinned her hair, and adjusted her kapp. She went back to the kitchen, where her mother was still busy at the stove. Without a word, Shelley set the table for four, lingering a few extra seconds by her father's place. She was grateful to have him home for meals, regardless of the fact that he rarely said more than a couple of words after the blessing.

"How is that new girl doing at the restaurant?" her mother asked, clearly trying to make small talk without making the conversation as personal as it had been.

Shelley played along. "Jocelyn? She seems fine, but she has a lot to learn."

"I can imagine. I guess I don't have to tell you how surprised everyone was that Joseph hired someone like her."

Shelley had been surprised at the time, too, but now that she knew Jocelyn better, she saw the softer side of the girl who used makeup and multicolored spiked hair as a barrier. "She's catching on very well, and the customers seem to like her."

"I'm surprised. She rather frightens me."

"Jocelyn isn't frightening at all. She's actually rather funny." Shelley smiled at the thought of some of Jocelyn's funny phrases.

Her mother looked at her with a lifted eyebrow and froze for a few seconds. "I hope you don't go getting any ideas that it's okay to dress or act like her."

Shelley laughed. "Trust me, Mother, I have no desire to do either of those things. But beneath her exterior, she's not as different from me as I thought at first."

William arrived home from school at that moment, a grin playing on his lips, even though he looked like he was trying to hide it. Shelley smiled back at him, and he looked away then laughed.

"Okay, so what are you so happy about?" Shelley asked.

"I asked Myra to marry me, and she said yes."

Chapter Seven

William's joy quickly vanished as their mother shrieked, "William! No!"

He took a step back, his face scrunching up as it always did before he cried. Shelley stood there in stunned silence as her mother told him he'd never be able to marry a girl. A huge tear trickled down his cheek, and his chin quivered.

When Mother stopped her rant, William looked her in the eye. "But I love her."

"You don't understand love," Mother replied.

He blinked and wiped a tear as it escaped. "I love you, too."

Mother looked helplessly at Shelley, silently pleading for help, but Shelley had no idea what to say. She understood her mother's concern, but she disagreed with her about William understanding love. He knew better than anyone how to love a person, but she was aware that didn't erase the complications of his proposal.

Shelley took a deep breath to steady her nerves and her voice before addressing her brother. "William, where do you know Myra?"

"She works with me at the shop."

"That settles it," their mother said. "You are not going back to that place. I told your father it wasn't a good idea for you to work."

"I want to keep working," William argued. "I like having my own money."

Shelley nodded. "I understand that, William." She glanced over at their mother. "Perhaps we can discuss this more, after Father gets home."

As Mother lifted her hand to her forehead, a sense of dread flooded Shelley. That simple gesture was generally followed by a quick drop into depression that could last for weeks. In the past, it seemed to be triggered by their father's switch to late shifts, but this was something new.

"William, you are awfully young to be thinking about getting married. How old is Myra?" Shelley asked.

He puffed up his chest and smiled. "Myra is eighteen years old." His grin widened. "And she's pretty. I like her red hair."

"I'm sure she's very pretty, but you haven't been working there very long. Getting married is very serious."

"I know that," William said. "I'm serious, too."

"Do you know anything about her family?"

"She lives in a group home."

"Does she have a family?"

He thought for a few seconds and then nodded. "I think her mother lives in Tampa. I don't know where her father lives."

Shelley and her mother exchanged a glance before Shelley turned back to William. "Maybe we can meet Myra sometime. Why don't I get someone to drive me to pick you up from work on Monday?"

"I like riding the van," he argued. "Myra rides with me, and we hold hands. We drop her off at her house first."

Shelley took a step back, placed her hands on her hips, and gave him what she hoped was an authoritative look. "Well, before you make the decision to marry Myra, we need to meet her and her family. I'm sure they feel the same way." She glanced at her mother, who stood off to the side looking aghast but remaining silent.

"Why?" he asked.

"That's just the way it's done. When you marry a girl, not only are you getting a wife, but you're also taking on her whole family."

"How about her? Does she get a whole new family, too?"

"Yes, William, it works both ways."

"That is very good. Myra says she wants a family just like mine, and now she'll have one."

Shelley hoped her talk hadn't backfired, but she couldn't worry about it. What she'd said was true, and now she needed to pray about it.

"Go wash up, William. Supper will be ready as soon as Father comes home."

As soon as he was out of the kitchen, Shelley's mother sank down in a chair. "What are we going to do?"

"We are going to pray, Mother. That's all we can do. Besides, William can't get married anyway because he's too young."

"You seem to be forgetting one very important thing, Shelley. William will never be able to get married."

Shelley wasn't so sure her mother was right, but even if she was, she was fretting over something unnecessarily. "I'll talk to William about all the things involved in getting married. Maybe he'll realize it's not as easy as he seems to think it is."

"I don't think he'll understand," Mother argued.

William understood quite a bit more than most people gave him credit for, and Shelley had been amazed at how much he comprehended. "Just let me talk to him before you worry any more. By the time I finish with him, I doubt he'll want to pursue this whole thing."

"Why?" Mother asked, her expression changing to confusion. "What do you plan to say to him?"

"I'm not sure yet. I'll need to think about it."

"Don't make him think marriage is a bad thing, just because you do."

Shelley was stunned. "I don't think marriage is bad. I think it's wonderful."

"If you think marriage is good, why aren't you trying harder to find a husband?"

Shelley's mouth went dry. Couldn't her mother see the truth—that getting married was extremely difficult for Shelley based on how much she was needed at home? She started to talk, but her voice caught in her throat. Good thing, too, because if she'd said what was on her mind, there was no telling how her mother would react.

"If your talk with William doesn't work, we have a mess on our hands. It's bad enough my oldest child married an outsider and left the church. To have my baby do that, too, and in his condition…" Her chin quivered just as William's had.

"Tammy is a very sweet woman," Shelley said. "They're going to church."

"But they're not going to our church, which was my dream. I always thought my children would grow up, get married, and attend the church you grew up in. That way we can always be together as a family, and I'd get to see my grandchildren."

"Mother, you get to see your grandchildren quite often, and it's not like they live all that far away. They always come when you need them. I pray every day that Paul comes back to our church and brings his family with him because I know it means so much to you." She took Mother's hand and held it tightly. Although Paul still walked with the Lord and attended a good church, her mother's heart was set on them being together as a family.

Her mother's eyes misted as she sighed and pulled her hand away. "Let's finish up supper so we can eat as soon as your father gets home."

As they worked in silence, Shelley allowed her thoughts to wander, and they settled on Jeremiah. Even though she'd seen some big changes in him, there was no way her mother would ever accept him. Shelley figured it was futile to even consider a relationship with him. Her mother would never forget that he'd left the church once, and she'd worry herself sick over the thought he might do it again. If he'd managed to continue walking with the Lord when he left, things might have been different, and her mother might have been more accepting.

Shelley was happy that he'd found a place with Abe though, even if she'd never be able to share it with him. She sighed and then startled as she realized the subconscious thoughts she'd been harboring. In spite of her words and attempts to keep her emotional distance from Jeremiah, she'd started to fall in love with him. That simply couldn't be. She'd hurt her family if she even suggested any such thing.

On Monday morning, Jeremiah worked hard at finishing the task Abe had assigned so he could start a little early on his own crops. Abe gave him a specific task each day now and told him that once it was done, he was free. Since he didn't need Charles today, he only had to be concerned about finishing his own work.

As he walked the rows of trees, he thought about

how closed off Shelley's family had seemed at church yesterday. After the services were over, the Burkholder family left before he'd had a chance to say more than good-bye to Mr. Burkholder and William. He'd seen Shelley across the room sitting in the midst of women, but she wouldn't look up at him.

"Good job, Jeremiah," Abe said from behind. "You look like a man on a mission."

"I am." Jeremiah suspected Abe only knew half the mission—the part about him having his own land. The other half was still in the works—the part with Shelley by his side as his wife. It would be a challenge, but that didn't deter Jeremiah. He'd overcome much more difficult tests, so he had no doubt he'd find a way to make Shelley realize how sincere he was.

"Do you need anything?"

"Not at the moment." At least not anything Abe could help him with.

"Good. Let me know when you're done."

After Abe took off toward another part of the property, Jeremiah let his mind wander to his personal life. During the time he'd been away from the church, he'd experienced myriad emotions, starting with a sense of freedom and ending with desperation for not being grounded anymore. How anyone could get through an entire life without their faith in God was beyond him. Not being connected with his church left him with an empty feeling. He had friends, but they could only do so much to satisfy the emptiness only the Lord could fill.

Once it became evident he needed to reconnect, he'd

fought God in his mind and by acting like someone he didn't know. He cringed as he remembered some of the things he'd shouted from his car when he'd seen Abe and Mary. Fortunately, they'd forgiven him and never even brought it up again. Now it was time for him to settle down and make a life for himself that was pleasing to God. He wanted a family, but he needed a wife who was interesting, intelligent, and could challenge him when he strayed in thought and word.

Shelley was perfect for him. He found her dedication to her family very attractive. Jeremiah was aware that he'd be taking on more than a wife if Shelley agreed to marry him, but he was fine with that. He liked William, and he was pretty sure William liked and respected him.

Now all he had to do was find a way to gain her family's trust. Her father was busy with his job, and her mother's emotional health seemed precarious, so it wouldn't be an easy feat. This would take considerable thought, but that was fine. He wasn't in a hurry.

After Shelley got off work on Monday afternoon, she walked to the church school. She knew that the van often waited at the school for William to get out of class, and she hoped that would be the case today. As soon as she got close enough to see the front, she saw that the van was there. She quickened her step until she approached the driver.

"Excuse me, but do you have room for one more person today?" she asked.

He turned and gave her a confused look. "I beg your pardon?"

Shelley explained that she wanted to go to William's workplace, but she didn't drive. He'd been in the area long enough to understand her situation.

"I think that would be fine, as long as it's just this once," he said. "A couple of the people are on vacation, so we're not full this week. This is my first stop, though. I still have a couple of stops to make."

"Good. Mind if I get in now?"

He opened the door for her, and she climbed into the very back seat. A few seconds after she buckled herself in, the front door of the school opened, and the kids streamed out. Only a couple of school-aged kids went to the shop where William worked, and William was the only one from the Pinecraft community, but the van was generally full at the end of the workday when the driver took everyone home. Shelley sat and waited for William to board the van. He didn't seem to notice her at first, but she said his name, and he turned around. At first he appeared happy to see her, and then his expression quickly changed.

"Why are you here, Shelley?" he asked. "Are you spying on me?"

"No, of course I'm not spying on you. I just want to see where you work and meet some of your friends."

"You just want to make trouble for me and Myra."

"I would never do that, but I do want to meet Myra. I'm sure she's a very nice girl."

"She's the nicest girl in the whole wide world. I love her."

"Then don't worry, William. I'm sure I'll love her, too."

They arrived at the shop a few minutes later. After the kids got out, Shelley hopped down from the van, turned around, and thanked the driver.

He waved. "I'll see you in a few hours."

"Do you have to go in with me?" William asked. "I don't want anyone to think I'm a baby."

"Why would anyone think you're a baby? You have a real job, so I'm sure they won't think that."

William looked uncomfortable before he finally said, "I want to tell Myra you're coming."

Shelley understood, so she told William to go on ahead of her. "I'll just walk around outside for a little while before I come back."

"You'll have to ask the man at the door to let you in. They are very strict about people coming into the building."

"Good," Shelley said. "I wouldn't want it any other way."

She made a lap around the building, thought about what she'd say and then walked up to the front door. Right after she opened it, she saw a man sitting on a stool behind a desk.

"I'd like to meet my brother's supervisor," she said.

The man looked her in the eye. "Do you know his name?"

Shelley knew he was inwardly laughing at her plain

clothes and kapp, but she didn't care. She was used to it. "Walter, I think. Walter…" She couldn't remember his last name.

"Walter O'Reilly?"

"*Ya*, that's his name. I'd like to see Walter O'Reilly."

The man picked up a phone and punched in a couple of numbers. After a few seconds he said something she couldn't hear, and then he placed his hand over the mouthpiece. "What did you say your name was?"

"Shelley Burkholder. I'm William Burkholder's sister." After the man said her name, he nodded, said, "I'll tell her," and then hung up. "He'll be right out to escort you to the workroom."

"Thank you." Shelley stood staring at the bare wall, feeling as awkward as she'd ever been. She rarely left the Pinecraft community, and now she remembered why. When one of the teachers at the school had recommended this job for William, the family had discussed the pros and cons and decided it would help him feel more valued and independent. Shelley knew her mother continued to have reservations, even after she'd agreed to let William work.

A few minutes later a man with a name tag that read O'Reilly came to the door. "So you're Willie's sister, huh? He said you were coming."

"*Ya*, I'm William Burkholder's sister." She regretted her decision to visit her brother at work, but it was too late now. "W—would it be all right if I saw his… um…work space?"

Mr. O'Reilly laughed but not in a mean way. He

gestured for her to join him. "That's perfectly fine. Right this way, ma'am." As they walked down a long corridor, he explained that the employees did mostly contracted piecemeal work for local businesses. They got a variety of jobs, including assembling simple components for factories and putting stickers on packages. "I've been doing this a very long time, and I can't think of a job I'd like more," he added with pride.

"Good," she said. "Everyone should enjoy their work."

They arrived beside a large, soft-peach painted, well-lit room with dozens of people similar to her brother, all working side by side, soft music playing in the background, some of the workers chattering with the person next to them. It seemed very pleasant.

"Where is William?" she asked.

"Follow me, and I'll show you."

She did as she was told and quickly found herself standing behind her brother, who still wasn't aware she was there yet. "William?"

He spun around and flashed a huge grin. He was about to say something when the girl to his right turned, looked at Shelley, and started laughing.

"What's so funny, Myra?" William asked.

"That woman. Look at that funny-looking outfit. It's so ugly."

Shelley was taken aback. Mr. O'Reilly touched her arm, but William stood from his chair, placed a hand on his hip, and shook a finger at Myra.

"That woman is my sister, and she is beautiful to me."

Myra continued laughing. "Not to me."

"How can you say that, Myra? I think she's beautiful."

"She is not beautiful. She's ugly."

Mr. O'Reilly stepped forward to intervene, but he stopped when Shelley shook her head and whispered, "I think it's best to let them work this out on their own."

William scowled. "That's mean. Take it back."

"No, I will not take it back. It's the truth."

"I don't want to marry you anymore then. I love my sister, and no one is allowed to say mean things about her to me."

Myra stopped laughing and then shrugged. "That's okay by me, William. I think you're sort of funny-looking, too."

Mr. O'Reilly looked just as surprised at Shelley felt. "In all the years I've been here, I've never seen anything like this happen. I am so sorry." He hung his head. "Myra hasn't been around many Mennonite or Amish people, I'm afraid. Her family isn't from here."

"Mr. O'Reilly, may I please be moved?" William asked. "I don't want to work next to Myra anymore."

"Yes, of course, Willie," Mr. O'Reilly said. He turned to Shelley with an apologetic look. "I'm so sorry this happened, but I really need to tend to my workers right now."

"Oh, please," Shelley said. "Go right ahead. I'll just stand here and observe if you don't mind."

Shelley stood and watched Mr. O'Reilly move her brother to the other side of the room. The two men carried his tools and equipment and placed it on an identical work space as far from Myra as they could go in the room. She wasn't sure what to think about what she'd just witnessed, but it clearly showed a side of William she'd never seen. He'd stuck up for her at the risk of his own happiness. Shelley couldn't remember ever being more proud of her brother than that very moment.

She turned back to see what Myra was doing. She half expected to see a shred of sadness, but what she saw was a silly young woman laughing with the guy on the other side of her. It didn't appear to Shelley that there was any deep love lost.

After Mr. O'Reilly finished helping William get set up in his new work space, he joined Shelley. "I feel bad that happened in front of you."

"Oh, don't feel bad. I'm flattered that my brother said what he did."

Mr. O'Reilly gave her a curious glance. "And I'm sorry about what Myra said about you. She apparently doesn't understand your style of dress. And by the way, I don't think you're ugly. You're actually rather attract—"

"That's okay," Shelley said, interrupting him before he said something to embarrass himself. "I've been laughed at before. People do that when they don't understand things, and unless they've been around plain people before, there's no way they would understand."

"You are a very wise young woman, Ms. Burkholder. May I get you something to drink?"

"No, thank you. I'll just go outside and wait for my

brother. The van driver said he had room to take me home."

"I have a better idea," Mr. O'Reilly said. "Come with me to the employee break room. We have magazines and comfortable seating."

"That sounds good." She followed him back out into the hallway and into another room—this one smaller and very cozy. It had thin carpet but a couple of plush couches on one side of the room, a coffee area with a refrigerator and small stove in the center, and on the other side a Ping-Pong table.

"I'll let William know you're here. He gets one very short break during his afternoon shifts."

Shelley leafed through a couple of cooking magazines. She'd never seen so many unusual foods. She closed a magazine, added it to the stack beside her, and was about to carry them back to the magazine rack and pick up a few more when William walked in.

"I'm sorry about what Myra said, Shelley."

"Don't worry about it, William. You had nothing to do with that."

He closed the distance between them and hugged her. "No one will ever be allowed to talk to my sister like that as long as I'm around."

Shelley's eyes misted. Having William protecting her warmed her heart and filled it with love.

"Want to play Ping-Pong?" he asked.

"I don't know how."

"Come on. I'll show you. But I only have a few minutes before I have to go back to work. Mr. O'Reilly let me take my break first because you are here."

Shelley tried to listen to her brother as he explained how to hit the ball and make it bounce to the other person, but her mind kept popping back to how quickly he did an about-face with Myra on her behalf. William was the most loyal person she'd ever known, and she was honored to be his sister.

The rest of the week went by quickly for Shelley. Her mother's eyes glistened with joy as she learned how William had stuck up for Shelley and not given it a second thought. Nothing else was mentioned about Myra, and William seemed fine with that.

As the days went by and Shelley didn't see Jeremiah, she tried to accept the idea that he might have given up. That was probably for the best, she thought, since her parents would probably never accept him.

Then on Friday, Jocelyn came up from behind her as she jotted down a big order and whispered, "Don't look now, but that cute guy who likes you just walked in."

Shelley felt her cheeks flame, but she did as Jocelyn told her and avoided looking toward the door. After she finished taking a late breakfast order, she scurried back to the kitchen without looking up.

"I'll take that," Mr. Penner said as he snatched the order slip from her hands. "Now go see what Jeremiah wants."

She opened her mouth to say Jocelyn could take his order, but Mr. Penner leveled her with a no-nonsense look. She clamped her mouth shut and nodded. She could tell Mr. Penner's attitude toward Jeremiah had changed.

As she approached Jeremiah's table, her heart hammered so hard she was certain he'd be able to hear it. She stopped beside his table, her pen poised above the order pad, and waited.

"Hello, Shelley."

He didn't say anything else, so she glanced up and met his gaze. His smile warmed her, but her mouth went dry.

"I've missed seeing you," he said. "But it takes quite a bit of time to work two farms."

"I can imagine," she said softly. "Would you like some coffee?"

He nodded. "Yes, please."

"I'll go get that for you right now while you decide what you'd like to eat."

"Sounds good."

Jocelyn met her at the beverage station. "I have to run to the courthouse to take care of a speeding ticket. Mr. Penner said I could go if I can get back in an hour, so I'd better run."

That left Shelley covering the entire dining room. "Can you be back before the lunch rush?"

"That's the plan." Jocelyn tweaked her on the arm and winked. "Better not keep the guy waiting." She laughed as she walked away.

Shelley carried a cup, a saucer, and a carafe filled

with coffee over to Jeremiah. "I'll be back with the cream," she said.

By the time she put the cream in front of Jeremiah, he had closed his menu. "Can you join me?"

"No, I'm sorry. I'm the only person serving at the moment."

"Too bad. I was hoping I could tell you all about my new crops."

"Maybe another time," Shelley said. "What would you like to eat?"

Jeremiah leaned back, folded his arms, and looked directly at her. "How about some pancakes and sausage?"

Fortunately, Jeremiah had worked hard all morning, so he'd worked up an appetite to eat another breakfast. Abe had wanted to talk to him when he'd first arrived at the Glick farm, so Mary had fed him eggs, bacon, hash browns, large buttermilk biscuits, and homemade marmalade, but then he'd done a couple of hours of hard manual labor.

He watched Shelley move around in the kitchen area doing whatever she did when she wasn't waiting on tables. The restaurant wasn't crowded because it was late for breakfast and early for lunch. He thought he'd timed his visit perfectly for Shelley's break, but with Jocelyn gone, he understood why she couldn't join him.

His order only took about ten minutes. Shelley had barely placed it in front of him when Mr. Penner came out of the kitchen, his face pale and his forehead scrunched with concern.

"I just got a call. There's been an accident," he said, his voice gravelly. "Jocelyn was taken by ambulance to the hospital."

Chapter Eight

"Come on, Mr. Penner," Jeremiah said as he rose from the table. "I'll take you to the hospital."

Mr. Penner glanced at Shelley. "Can you handle the dining room all by yourself?"

"Of course," she said. "Go on and see about Jocelyn."

Shelley remained standing beside the table as the two men left for the hospital. Then she bowed her head and prayed for her coworker with a bad driving record.

The restaurant wasn't so crowded that Shelley couldn't handle it alone. She even had a little bit of time between taking orders and delivering meals to straighten the beverage and prep area.

Mr. Penner and Jeremiah came back right when the lunch crowd started to roll in. "How is she?"

Mr. Penner smiled. "She has a mild concussion, so they're keeping her overnight for observation. She wants to come back to work tomorrow, but I told her absolutely not. I want her to take better care of herself."

He gestured to Jeremiah. "Let's get this boy some food so he can get back to the farm."

Shelley had cancelled Jeremiah's breakfast order, and now he wanted lunch. It didn't take long for the kitchen staff to prepare the food. When she delivered it to his table, he told her more about Jocelyn's accident.

"Apparently, she ran a red light and hit a truck, according to what she remembers."

"Oh no! Was anyone else hurt?"

Jeremiah shook his head. "Fortunately, she tried to stop, so the truck driver is okay. Jocelyn really does need to slow down."

"Thank you for taking Mr. Penner to the hospital. He cares about people."

"Yes, I know," Jeremiah agreed. "Including you."

"*Ya.* I've been working for him since I was in high school. I feel like part of his family."

A family walked into the restaurant, so Shelley left Jeremiah's table to take care of their order. For the next several minutes she was busy, but Jeremiah waited.

When he lifted his finger to get her attention, she went to his table. "May I have my check, please? I need to get back to the farm."

"*Neh.* Mr. Penner said you don't need to worry about paying for lunch. He's thankful you were here to help him."

Jeremiah hesitated for a second and then nodded. "I'm happy to do it. Tell him thank you from me. I'll be back soon, and I'd like to talk with you."

Shelley opened her mouth, but she couldn't think

of anything to say, so she smiled and nodded. After he left, she tried to get her mind off Jeremiah, but that was impossible. She could see that he'd truly changed since he'd come back to the church, and she liked what she saw. She'd secretly liked him when they were children, but he'd pulled so many pranks and teased her that she couldn't bring herself to let on how she felt. They'd actually started getting along as teenagers, and she'd harbored thoughts that perhaps he was the boy she'd wind up with. Then he'd turned his back on the church, leaving little hope that he'd ever come back. That was when she'd turned to Peter, who'd seemed safe.

As Shelley and Peter had seen more of each other, she'd placed all her hopes on a future with him. He'd acted as though he wanted more, but when he'd shocked her with the news he was engaged to Clara from Pennsylvania, she'd doubted she would ever find a man to spend her life with.

"Shelley," Mr. Penner said from behind her. "I just got a call from Jeremiah. He offered to take you to visit Jocelyn after work if you are able to go."

She thought about how her mother wouldn't approve, but then she really wanted to let Jocelyn know she was praying for her. "I would like that," she said softly. "But I offered to help the kids at the school get ready for the singing on Sunday."

"How long will that take you?"

"Maybe an hour?"

"I'll let him know to pick you up after you are finished at the school."

Her thoughts collided and then swirled in her head. She wanted to see Jocelyn, but her parents wouldn't approve of her riding with Jeremiah.

Mr. Penner studied her face. "Jeremiah likes you very much, Shelley. At first I worried that he would be bad for you, but he seems to be a changed man."

Shelley glanced at him and saw the twinkle in his eyes, so she quickly looked away. "I hope so."

"May I tell him you will accept the ride to the hospital?"

She nodded. "*Ya*, I would like to see Jocelyn, but I have to go to the church and help out with the children first."

"I will let him know you said yes. Abe told him it was okay to take the time off, so I will let you leave early, and maybe you can get a head start with the children."

"Thank you." As soon as Shelley could walk away from Mr. Penner without being rude, she did.

The combination of her growing feelings for Jeremiah and the desire to see Jocelyn had Shelley swirling in a current of emotions. She needed to settle her mind before she could hope to make sense of all the changes going on. If Jeremiah truly was a changed man, she thought about whether or not she could be with him. Her mother's lack of acceptance combined with her own fears of having something else taken away made her wary. Keeping trust in anything outside her faith, family, and work was becoming more difficult by the day.

The lunch crowd kept her busy for a couple of hours, so when Jeremiah arrived to take her to the school and hospital, she wasn't quite ready. "I thought you were picking me up at the school."

"I finished early."

"It'll be a few minutes before I'm done here."

"I'll wait," he said as he stood by the door. "Take your time, and finish your work."

She was wiping a table clean when Mrs. Penner walked in the front door. "Go on, Shelley. I'm taking over for you."

Shelley knew it had been years since Mrs. Penner had waited tables at the restaurant, so she hesitated. "I don't—"

Mrs. Penner made a shooing gesture, shushing Shelley. Jeremiah stood to the side observing everything.

Jeremiah opened the passenger door for Shelley. As she got in and strapped her seat belt around her tiny frame, he felt more protective of her than ever. He wanted to protect her from anything bad ever happening, but she had a shield that he couldn't seem to get past. Sure, she was nice to him, and she didn't seem to mind making small talk. But he wanted so much more.

"Did you see Jocelyn yet?" Shelley asked, breaking him from his thoughts.

"Just for a few seconds. Mr. Penner went in first, and he talked to her for a while before he came and got me. When the doctor arrived, we both had to leave."

"Is she…does she look the same?"

"With the exception of a few bruises and a scratch over her eye, she looks exactly as she always looked." He left out how Jocelyn's tough-girl exterior had faded, and she looked vulnerable and frightened. "And I have no doubt she'll be very happy to see you." Although he didn't know Jocelyn well, he couldn't miss her when he'd gone to Penner's.

"I like Jocelyn. She works hard and says funny things."

Jeremiah thought about all the girls he'd met when he was away from the church. Many of them had taken on an image of what they wanted the world to see and kept their innermost thoughts hidden. He knew it was a protective measure, but he didn't like it. And he suspected God didn't care for it either.

"I will wait in the back of the church," Jeremiah said as he pulled up to the curb in front.

Shelley went to the classroom and asked if they could start early. The teachers were happy she was there, so they gathered the kids to herd them to the front of the church sanctuary.

The children must have sensed Shelley's anxiety, and they started acting out. One of the younger boys made faces at the girl behind him.

"Turn around, and keep your hands to yourself, Zeke," Shelley said, her voice tight and on edge.

Zeke turned around, but he still didn't pay attention to her. Instead he jumped around, flailing his arms. Then the boy next to him began to squirm, creating a snowball effect with the rest of the children. This was the first time Jeremiah had ever seen Shelley lose control. He couldn't sit back and do nothing.

"Okay, that's enough." Jeremiah's booming voice behind Shelley caught the attention of the children. "Do you want to make Miss Burkholder, your parents, and the rest of the church members happy by showing your hard work and dedication, or do you want to look like a bunch of people who didn't practice when it comes time to sing?"

Zeke burst out in laughter, but he quickly stopped when Jeremiah leveled him with a stern look. Shelley stood transfixed as Jeremiah continued to lecture for a few more minutes. Finally, he turned to Shelley and motioned for her to come forward.

"Miss Burkholder, I think they're ready to settle down and get to work now," Jeremiah said as he took a step back.

She turned and gave him a private smile and then resumed singing practice. The children were perfectly behaved, enabling them to finish very quickly.

Afterward the teachers brought them back to their classrooms, and Shelley looked up at Jeremiah. "Thank you for helping me. I normally don't have that much trouble with them."

"I know. You normally do quite well with children. Kids sense when adults have something else on their minds."

They pulled up in front of the hospital entrance. "Why don't you go on up to see her?" he said. "I'll park the car and hang out in the waiting room until you're ready to go home." He gave her directions to Jocelyn's unit and then watched her until she disappeared through the automatic double doors.

Shelley hadn't changed much since they were younger. She'd always been responsible, intelligent, and straightforward. The only difference between then and now was her guardedness, which he suspected was related to issues with her mother, Peter, and possibly her brother William.

Shelley's hands shook as she followed the nurse to Jocelyn's hospital room. The sounds of medical machines whirring and buzzing made her uneasy. She'd visited people in the hospital before, but the shock of the differences from her regular life never went away.

"Here she is," the nurse said as she opened the door. "The doctor says she's doing well, so take your time, and have a nice visit."

Shelley walked slowly into the room toward Jocelyn. With the sun shining through the window behind Jocelyn, it was difficult to see her features, so her injuries weren't evident until Shelley was right beside the bed. Even then, she didn't look as banged up as she'd expected.

"Hey there, Shelley. Who's minding the shop?"

She certainly sounded like Jocelyn—not some feeble, injured person. "Mrs. Penner came in to help out so I could come here."

Jocelyn belted out a laugh and then stopped and raised her hand to her head. "Ouch. It hurts to laugh."

"Then don't do it," Shelley said. "I don't want you to hurt."

"I couldn't help it. It's hard to imagine Mrs. Penner waiting on tables and putting up with some of the… well, you know how the customers can be."

Shelley nodded and grinned. "Yes, I do know, but I think Mrs. Penner can handle it. She used to work there every day when I was younger. I'm sure she'll be just fine."

"So I guess you're probably wondering what happened," Jocelyn said.

"I heard you hit a truck."

"Yeah. I was going too fast, and I couldn't slow down for the light. Ironic, huh?"

Shelley tilted her head in confusion. "Ironic?"

"That I was speeding to the courthouse to pay a speeding ticket, and that's what got me into trouble. Can you believe that I got another ticket?"

"Will you be able to drive again?" Shelley asked.

"Oh, I have to drive. It's too hard to get around without wheels." Jocelyn caught herself and chuckled softly. "But I guess you know that."

"It's not all that difficult," Shelley said. "I like walking, and when I need a ride, I take the bus or hire a driver."

Jocelyn turned away, and silence fell between them. When she faced Shelley again, her face had an odd expression that Shelley had never seen before.

"So tell me what it's like to be you," Jocelyn said.

"What do you mean?"

Jocelyn gestured toward what Shelley was wearing. "I mean to wear that getup all the time and never put on makeup. You always have that little thingy on your head, and your hair is always up in a knot. And that long skirt. Does it ever bug you?"

"Bug me?"

"Yeah. Doesn't it make you nuts to never wear shorts or let your hair down or play up your eyes with some fabulous makeup?" Jocelyn leaned forward a bit. "I mean, you have some killer peepers that would look amazing with a little mascara."

Shelley was slightly puzzled by some of the words, but she caught the gist of what Jocelyn was saying. "*Neh*, it doesn't bother me. This is all I know."

"Well," Jocelyn said as she leaned back and fidgeted with the sheet. "That is true. If you've never experienced anything else, you wouldn't know what you were missing." She pursed her lips before adding, "And to be truthful, I don't think you're really missing all that much."

Shelley didn't know how to respond to that. She walked over toward the window and glanced out over the parking lot.

"I want to go back to work tomorrow, but the doc says I need to wait until he clears me. He's letting me go home tomorrow though, so I can pretty much do whatever I want."

Shelley turned back around to face Jocelyn. "Don't rush things."

"You're too young to be my mom, but I appreciate

the maternal advice. I haven't had that since my mom found someone else and took off, leaving me and my dad to figure out how to be a family, just the two of us."

"Is your father…um, does he know about your accident?"

"Yeah, he knows, but he's been pretty busy lately, so I don't expect to see him anytime soon."

Shelley made some uncomfortable small talk for a few minutes before backing toward the door. "I really need to go now. My mother likes me to help with dinner. I'm glad you're doing well enough to go home tomorrow, but I don't want you to push yourself too hard. Mrs. Penner and I can manage until you're feeling better."

Jocelyn laughed and waved. "Have fun, but don't forget about me. I need that job. It's hard finding a new one these days."

"Don't worry. We won't forget about you. I'm sure Mrs. Penner will be very happy when you return."

As Shelley walked toward the waiting room, where Jeremiah said he'd be waiting, she thought about some of the things Jocelyn had said, particularly the comment about not missing something she'd never experienced. As much as she noticed the changes in Jeremiah, she wondered if he'd miss his experiences from his more worldly life as her mother had said he might. She now realized that was the source of much of her fear of getting too close to him. What if he missed it so much he decided to leave the church again?

Jeremiah stood and smiled as she approached. "Ready to leave now?"

Shelley nodded and then averted her gaze. They walked without talking, the only sounds coming from the machines in the hospital and their shoes clopping on the floor.

"Wait here, and I'll go get the car," he said after they reached the double doors leading to the outside.

"*Neh*, I'll walk with you."

"I don't mind," he said.

"There's no use in standing around waiting for you when I'm perfectly capable of walking." She stepped down off the curb.

After they were buckled into Jeremiah's car, he put his key in the ignition and turned. The car made a little groan and then thudded.

Shelley looked at Jeremiah. His face was scrunched up with concern. "I was afraid this might happen."

"What's going on?" Shelley had so little experience with cars—she wasn't sure if this was serious.

"Abe told me that if I insisted on having a car, I didn't need one as fancy or with as much power as the sports car I got rid of. I chose this one just to have transportation. It's a clunker."

"Are you blaming Abe? It's not his fault."

"No, of course I'm not blaming Abe. I'm the one who knows about cars. I worked in an automotive shop before Abe hired me, so I take full responsibility."

"In that case, can't you fix it?"

Jeremiah shook his head as he raked his fingers

through his closely cropped hair. "No, I don't think there's anything I can do to fix this old heap. I bought it really cheap so I could pay cash, and I didn't have that much money to work with." He leaned back and shook his head. "I have some decisions to make, and it looks like it'll happen sooner rather than later."

"The first decision is how we're going to get home," Shelley said. "I think the bus comes out here."

"It does," Jeremiah said. "But I don't want you having to take the bus."

"Why not?" she asked. "I don't mind."

Jeremiah lifted his hand and started to pound his fist on the steering wheel, but his Mennonite sensibilities kicked in just in time. He took a couple of deep breaths to settle his nerves. "I s'pose I could leave my car here and escort you home."

"Why?" She narrowed her eyes. "I can ride the bus alone."

"Yes, I know, but"—he opened his car door—"but I have to go home, too, and I don't live that far from you, so we might as well ride together."

"What will you do about the car?"

"I'll have to call someone to tow it to a junkyard."

After they got out of the car, Jeremiah stood looking at it for a few seconds before turning to walk away. Shelley didn't follow, so he glanced around to see what she was doing.

"What's wrong?" he asked.

She looked back and forth between Jeremiah and his

car. He waited for a few seconds, hoping she'd catch up, but she didn't.

"Okay, Shelley, I can tell you're thinking about something you're not saying. What is it?"

"Since your car isn't working anymore, and you said it isn't worth fixing, why don't you try going without a car?"

"You're kidding, right?"

She tossed him a puzzled look. "Kidding?"

"Are you saying you expect me to live without my own wheels?"

"*Ya.* That's exactly what I'm saying."

"Abe has already challenged me to do that, but I'm not sure I'm ready just yet." Jeremiah looked around the hospital parking lot at the sea of cars. "That is an extremely difficult step to take."

"Maybe it'll be difficult at first, but I do just fine."

"Let's check with the hospital receptionist and find out where the closest bus stop is."

After she directed them to the location where they could catch the bus, they walked outside and resumed their conversation. Shelley spoke first.

"You might discover you don't need a car," she said.

She'd obviously never understand, so Jeremiah didn't want to argue with her. "Maybe. Looks like I don't have a choice, and I'll have to make do for a while—at least until I make enough money to buy a newer automobile. In the meantime, I'll go back to walking and catching rides whenever I can." Jeremiah paused before adding, "And I guess I'd better set something up with David."

"David?"

"Yeah, the guy Abe hires to drive him places that are too far to walk. Until I get my house built on the farm, I'll need him twice a day. That can wind up costing me some money."

"Will it be more than what you pay for in gas?"

Jeremiah mentally calculated the cost of gas, maintenance, and insurance. "It might actually cost a little less if David will cut me a deal."

Shelley smiled. "That would be nice."

The bus ride to Pinecraft was uneventful. There were only a few people seated toward the front, and the bus was able to go past all stops except one where a young woman waited. As they took the last step onto the sidewalk, the bus driver wished them a good day and took off.

In spite of Shelley telling Jeremiah she could walk from the bus stop to her house, he insisted on getting off the bus with her, escorting her home, and walking the three blocks to his house. They had to dodge a couple of children playing in their yards. Memories of Jeremiah's own childhood flickered through his mind, and nostalgia nearly overwhelmed him.

"What are you thinking about?" Shelley asked as they rounded the corner to her street. "You seem mighty pensive."

He shrugged. "Just about how those kids remind me of myself when I was their age."

"I remember you back then. You were quite a character."

Jeremiah laughed. "Yeah, I was, wasn't I?"

"You used to tease me unmercifully."

"That was because I liked you," he said, a grin quirking the corners of his lips.

"If that's how you act when you like a girl, I wouldn't want to see what you do when you don't like her."

"There aren't many people I don't like," Jeremiah said.

Shelley's mother stood near the door as Shelley entered the house. "Where have you been? I expected you home a long time ago."

"Jocelyn was injured in a car accident, so I went to the hospital to see her."

"You should have come home first to tell me so I wouldn't worry. It is dangerous for a young girl like you to be trotting about in an area you're not familiar with."

"I wasn't alone," Shelley said. She cringed as she added, "Jeremiah was with me."

She braced herself for an outburst of all of Jeremiah's faults. She was surprised her mother's expression softened.

"That's good. At least he knows the ways of the world, and he will protect you." She started to walk toward the kitchen, but she stopped and turned to face Shelley. "How is Jocelyn?" Shelley told her mother about the concussion and how Jocelyn would probably be back at work soon. She was surprised not to get a lecture about the evils of living in the world.

William came home shortly afterward, and Father followed. As they sat down at the table, Shelley looked around at her family and wondered what it would be like to have her own family. Then she sighed as she considered the unlikelihood that that would happen. Even if a man was in love with her, taking on the responsibility of William might make him think twice before committing to her for life. In many ways, William was easier to contend with than someone without Down syndrome. He rarely argued, and with very few exceptions, he seemed eager to please.

When Shelley started to bring up Jocelyn's accident, her mother grimaced and gestured not to discuss it. After dinner, when William and their father had left the kitchen, Shelley turned to her mother.

"Why didn't you want me to talk about Jocelyn?" she asked.

Her mother didn't look directly at her. "We don't know much about Jocelyn, and I didn't want to upset your father."

Shelley suspected it had nothing to do with her father and everything to do with the fact that her mother didn't want to constantly be reminded about Shelley's brother Paul leaving the church. The instant she thought that, it dawned on her that this was the same issue with Jeremiah. Having him around was a reminder.

"Mother, do you ever talk with Paul about his faith?"

Her mother's expression hardened. "Paul's faith—or

lack of it—has broken my heart, so I don't want you to ever bring it up again."

"I just—"

"You heard me. Paul's faith is not open for discussion."

Shelley held up her hands. "Okay, I won't talk about it anymore if it upsets you that much." She carried the last of the serving dishes to the sink. "William seems to be doing well, considering he and Myra—"

"Leave the kitchen, Shelley."

"But, Mother—"

Her mother stabbed her finger in the direction of the door to the rest of the house. "I told you to leave. I cannot discuss this any longer."

Shelley did as she was told. The tension in the house was almost more than she could bear. William glanced up from the couch, where he sat as her father read from the Bible. His smile quickly faded as their gazes met.

"Are you mad at someone?" he asked.

Shelley shook her head as she bit back tears. All she'd wanted to do was have a meaningful conversation with her mother, but she kept getting shut out because her mother couldn't face things she didn't like.

Father put down the Bible and looked back and forth between Shelley and William. "Why don't the two of you go out for some ice cream?"

William hopped up and clapped his hands. "Let's go, Shelley. I want some rocky road ice cream."

Chapter Nine

Jeremiah still hadn't replaced his car two weeks after his old one died. He'd found a junkyard that would pay him a small amount as well as tow it from the hospital parking lot. He was surprised it hadn't cost him money. He'd gone looking at other cars, but Shelley's words continued ringing through his mind. Somehow he'd managed quite well without having his own wheels. It wasn't nearly as difficult to adjust to his old lifestyle as he'd thought.

He turned around and worked on another section of ground, getting it ready for a new variety of oranges Abe wanted to plant. He felt a trickle of sweat drip down his back. Summer had arrived early this year.

"How's the planting going?" Abe asked.

Jeremiah tossed the shovelful of dirt to the side. "I'm almost finished digging this row."

"I'm talking about on your land."

Jeremiah straightened and leaned against the shovel.

"I have most of the summer crop planted already, so now it's just a matter of weeding while I wait."

"*Ya*, that is what we have to do."

"I've been thinking about where to put a house," Jeremiah said. "I know it needs to go over by the cluster of trees, but any advice you have would be appreciated."

Abe offered a clipped nod. "We can discuss that soon. For now, I'd like you to help me unload some of the trees I just had delivered."

Jeremiah followed Abe to the truck parked at the end of the long shell-covered road that forked in two directions—one going to the house and the other to the edge of the grove. Jeremiah couldn't help but smile as he thought about how he'd have a place of his own like this one of these days.

"It might start raining soon," Abe said. "That would be good for the newly transplanted trees."

Jeremiah glanced up at the sky. It was a deep blue with a few puffs of fluffy white clouds hanging low. He didn't see any sign of rain, but whenever Abe said rain was coming, he was generally right.

They worked hard for the rest of the afternoon, finishing a few minutes before the first clap of thunder. "I hope we get a soaker," Abe said. "That will get the trees off to a nice start." He started toward his house. "Come on inside before it starts pouring."

Jeremiah followed Abe to the house. They were dampened by the first drops of rain, but they made it to the front porch before the downpour.

Mary joined them, and they stood and watched the

rain for a few minutes before she finally spoke up. "I talked to Shelley a couple of days ago. I wish someone had called me, so I could help while Jocelyn was out."

Jeremiah suspected that Mr. Penner didn't want to bother Mary, so he hadn't called to let her know. "Your grandmother filled in."

A wry smile tweaked Mary's mouth. "That must have been interesting."

"Did Shelley say anything about it?" Jeremiah asked.

"No, she wouldn't." Mary glanced over at Abe, who continued to gaze out at the rain. "I have never heard Shelley complain about anything or anyone."

"Not even me?"

"Why would she complain about you?" Mary's eyes twinkled as she laughed. "I'm the one who did all the complaining about you."

"You know I'm very sorry about that."

"*Ya*, I do know that, and you know all is forgiven."

Jeremiah leaned against one of the poles on the porch. "Shelley challenged me to give up my car for good."

Abe whipped around, his eyebrows lifted. "So is that why you aren't driving a car anymore—to make Shelley happy?"

With the question put that way, Jeremiah immediately knew the answer. "No. She got me thinking about it, but since I'm renewing my commitment to the Lord and coming back to the church, I figured it was time to stop dipping my toes into the water and just take the plunge."

Mary laughed again. "The way you talk reminds me of some of my old customers, Jeremiah."

Abe cast a glance at Mary. "I find it rather strange."

"Strange isn't always bad," Mary said. "I think it's fun."

Jeremiah remembered a time when Mary didn't feel that way. Abe had been good for her by accepting who she was and loving everything about her. When Jeremiah first came to Abe to discuss coming back to the church, Abe's protectiveness toward Mary had been the only obstacle Jeremiah had had to overcome. Jeremiah still felt bad about the taunting and rude comments he'd hollered from his car. Mary deserved so much better than that. Fortunately, she was as kindhearted as Abe, and she'd forgiven him.

"Jeremiah?" Mary's sweet voice startled him. "Are you feeling okay?"

He shook himself. "I'm doing just fine. Every once in a while I get lost in my thoughts."

She grinned. "Love has a way of doing that to you."

"What are you talking about, Mary?" Abe asked.

Mary turned her smiling face toward her husband. "Jeremiah knows what I'm talking about, right?"

Of course he did, but he decided to change the subject rather than field questions he didn't have answers to. "With David being available to drive me back and forth to work, I think I can do just fine without an automobile."

"Ya," Abe agreed. "That is what I've been trying to tell you."

"It took my car breaking down to get it through my thick skull, but God is in control," Jeremiah said.

"Since it's still raining, how about coming inside? Mary asked me to repair a few things in the house. Maybe you can give me a hand."

"Yes, of course," Jeremiah answered. "I'll be glad to help with anything you need."

As he walked past Mary on the porch, he tried not to look directly at her knowing, smiling face. She was extremely astute, and he suspected she was aware of everything he was thinking—particularly when he harbored thoughts of Shelley.

The following Sunday Shelley had a difficult time getting William out of bed. Worry gnawed at her stomach as she shook his shoulder. He mumbled something she couldn't quite understand.

"Are you sick?" she asked.

"He's not sick," her mother said from the doorway. "That awful girl Myra upset him yesterday at his company's picnic."

Shelley's heart twisted. "Don't let anyone upset you this much, William. You might have thought you were in love with Myra, but if she's mean to you, she's not worth being upset over."

William turned his head toward Shelley to face her. As he opened his eyes, she could tell he'd been crying. "Everyone was laughing at me," he said, his voice hoarse. "I don't like it when people laugh at me."

"They are stupid people," their mother said sternly.

Shelley placed her hands on William's shoulders. "People laugh at others when they don't know what else to do."

"It makes my stomach hurt when people laugh at me," William said, sniffling.

Shelley knew exactly what he was talking about. She'd experienced it when she was younger and went places where people didn't understand the plain way of life. It had taken years to eventually tune out the ignorant people who made fun of anyone unlike them.

"Stop feeling sorry for yourself, William," Mother said as she backed away from the door. "Church starts in one hour. Get up and get ready." Without another word she walked away.

"Shelley, what can I do to make her stop being so mean?" William asked.

"Try to ignore her," Shelley replied, wishing she had a better answer that would soothe him and make Myra stop. But she knew there was no simple answer. "Eventually, she'll stop when she discovers her words aren't getting the reaction she wants."

William slowly sat up in bed and used the edge of the sheet to dab at his eyes. "Will Jeremiah be at church today?"

Shelley froze. She hadn't seen much of Jeremiah since the day his car wouldn't start. She understood how difficult it must have been to give up the freedom from having his own car, but she'd hoped he'd make more of an effort to stop by the restaurant. In spite of her thoughts that he might not be good for her, she'd started looking forward to seeing him. After her experience with Peter leading her on and then announcing he planned to marry Clara, she'd erected a shield around her heart. Jeremiah had managed to bring back some feelings she wasn't sure she'd ever have again.

William waved his hand in front of Shelley's face to get her attention. "Well? Will he?"

"I—I would assume so." Shelley stood and eased away from the bedside. "Now get up, and start getting ready. At least we know Myra won't be at church, so you don't need to worry about her today."

William grinned. "Good thing for that."

"Yes, it's a very good thing. I have to help Mother finish making the salad and rolls for the potluck after church."

"Are you making dessert?"

"Not this time. Last potluck we had too many desserts and not enough salads."

William grinned and rubbed his tummy. "I like dessert."

She flashed a smile as she closed William's door so he could get ready. Fortunately, William had forgotten his humiliation—at least temporarily. As she walked toward the kitchen, she said a silent prayer that God would find something else for Myra to think about so William would have some peace. It was bad enough for him to have to ward off Myra's jeers about the way Shelley dressed.

Her mother didn't waste a second. The instant Shelley arrived in the kitchen her mother started issuing orders, which was just fine. It kept Shelley from having to think about William, Jeremiah, or herself.

"Where's Father?" Shelley asked.

"He went on ahead to the church. Some of the men wanted to get the grounds ready for our potluck early." She cast a frown at Shelley. "William was supposed to go with him, but your father couldn't make him budge."

Shelley needed to change the subject quickly. "This salad looks delicious."

"Do me a favor, and put the rolls in that basket over there. I'll cover them with one of the clean dish towels in the drawer."

By the time they finished getting everything together, William had joined them in the kitchen. "I'm starving."

"I set some ham and a biscuit by the stove," their mother said. "Better hurry and eat because we need to get going."

Fifteen minutes later, the three of them were on their way to church. William carried the basket of rolls, while Shelley and Mother brought the salad and the ingredients they'd have to add at the last minute.

The second the church came into view, Shelley saw Jeremiah. He stood by the corner of the building, watching in her direction.

"That boy!" Shelley's mother shook her head. "Why isn't he working with the other men?"

"Maybe they're finished," William said. "Lookee over there. Father's standing around talking to his friends."

Their mother's scowl let Shelley know that no matter what Jeremiah did, it wouldn't be good enough. Too bad Shelley's pulse had taken on a life of its own. She could feel her heart beating from the top of her head to the tips of her toes.

Before Shelley even got to the church property, Jeremiah was on his way to them. "Here," he said as he reached for the oversized bowl in her mother's hands. "Let me carry that for you."

Shelley half expected her mother to yank it away and say she didn't need his help. But she didn't. Instead, she pointed to the side of the church. "That goes in the kitchen. See to it you don't get distracted by anyone along the way."

Jeremiah cut his eyes toward Shelley and made a goofy face. She had to bite the insides of her cheeks to keep from laughing.

Mother jumped in right behind Jeremiah, preventing Shelley from directly following him, clearly a method of keeping them from being too close. Jeremiah placed the bowl where he was told. After he turned around, he leaned to make eye contact with Shelley. Her face flamed as her mother spun around and glared at her.

Mrs. Penner chose that moment to appear. "Melba! I'm so glad you remembered the salad. Looks like we have too many desserts again. Come with me, and let's see if we can figure out a way to space them better, so the children won't get too carried away with the sweets."

Shelley watched as her mother made a decision be-

tween remaining between her and Jeremiah or follow-
ing Mrs. Penner. The quick look her boss's wife gave
Shelley let her know she had intervened on purpose.
Shelley gulped.

"Oh…" Mother turned a frown on Shelley but softened her facial features as she nodded to Mrs. Penner.
"Okay. Shelley, make sure William is taken care of and
seated before you join the women."

Shelley watched her mother and Mrs. Penner weave
their way through the group toward the food that was
already set up. She tingled at the awareness of Jeremiah standing so close.

"Your mother loves you," Jeremiah said, "and she's
trying to protect you."

"Protect me?" Shelley blinked before looking at Jeremiah. "From what?"

"From me. She obviously still doesn't trust me, and
I can't say I don't blame her. I'll probably do the same
thing with my daughter…if the Lord chooses to bless
me with one."

Shelley knew he was right, but she didn't want to
continue with this conversation, which took her to an
uncomfortable place in her heart. "It looks like we'll
have plenty of food for the potluck."

Jeremiah tilted his head back and laughed. "Was
there ever a time when we didn't? The women in this
church like to make sure everyone is well fed."

"And what is wrong with that?"

"Nothing." Jeremiah grimaced. "Why do I feel like
I said the wrong thing?"

Shelley sighed. "You didn't. I didn't mean to come across so harsh. It's just that…well, I don't know what to say right now."

"You could say that you will go to the museum with me when I have some time off from work."

Now she was totally speechless. When she tried to think of a response, nothing came to mind.

Jeremiah gave her a look of understanding. "Think about it. I'll stop by the restaurant next week, and we can talk about it then."

She nodded.

"I'd better go help the men finish setting up the tables, or they'll send out a search party for me."

Shelley watched Jeremiah walk away to join the group of men pulling tables out of the church and setting them up on the lawn. Exerting their wisdom and authority, the older men directed the younger ones. She was happy to see William pitching in and carrying chairs. He'd managed to overcome his own sadness to help others. Shelley sent up a short prayer of thanks for her younger brother.

As Shelley worked with the women, she occasionally cast a glance over toward the men. A few times she noticed Jeremiah talking to William and explaining something to him. The sight of William being treated like a man was comforting and elevated Jeremiah in her mind. She wondered if her mother noticed this.

Throughout the church service, Shelley resisted the urge to look at Jeremiah. She didn't want her mother to think he was pulling her away from her faith. When she was sure her mother wouldn't notice, she stole a glance in Jeremiah's direction and saw that he and William were leaning into each other. Father was on the other side of William, clearly oblivious to his own son's affection for Jeremiah.

Shelley thought about how she'd be with her own children. She'd certainly try to care about their feelings and innermost thoughts without trying to impose her own dreams for them. After church was over, Mother didn't waste a single second. She took Shelley by the hand and pulled her toward the room where the food was stored. "We need to get the salads, vegetables, casseroles, and meats outside right away, or the men and children will think they can start with dessert."

Shelley seriously doubted that most of the men would do that, but she went along with her mother. Every few minutes she caught herself looking for Jeremiah. When she spotted him, a sense of satisfaction and gladness washed over her.

As soon as the food tables were full, the pastor said the blessing. There was a brief stampede toward the tables, with the younger men claiming their spots first in line, followed by the older men and children. The women hung back until the lines dwindled, and then they filled their plates. There was never any concern about not having enough food because most families brought enough to feed more than the people they came with.

Shelley had a very small appetite, so she didn't pile her plate with as much as she normally did. Before she sat, she took another look in Jeremiah's direction. William was about to sit next to him. She hoped Jeremiah didn't mind; it looked as though he was fine with William clinging to his side.

Mother, Mrs. Penner, Mary, and a couple of the other women were clustered around one end of a large table for twelve. Shelley assumed the empty chair next to Mary was for her, but she asked before sitting.

Mary pulled the chair back. "I saved the seat for you." Mary looked at Shelley's plate and grinned. "Oh good. I see that you got some of my ambrosia. Abe says it's the best he's ever tasted, so I thought it would be good for today." She leaned over and cupped her mouth as she whispered, "It's the recipe the cook at my grandparents' restaurant uses, but Abe says mine's better."

Shelley scooped up a bite of the ambrosia and tasted it. "I think it's better, too. Did you put something extra in it?"

Mary shrugged. "Just a tad more sugar, maybe, and an extra handful of coconut."

Shelley laughed. "Then this is a Mary Glick original. You have turned out to be a very good cook. I would never have thought to change a recipe."

"I can't imagine following any instructions precisely as they are written. Where's the fun in that?"

Shelley couldn't imagine not following directions for fear of a disaster. "Everything you attempt turns out better than the original."

Mary snickered and shook her head. "You only say that because I don't share the flops. And there are plenty of them." The changes in Mary since Shelley had met her were phenomenal. When Mary first came to the school nearly ten years ago, she had a perpetual scowl on her face. Shelley suspected Mary had been shy but covered it by acting as though she didn't care about making friends. In spite of that, Shelley had forced herself upon Mary, and they gradually grew to be as close as Mary would allow. Some of the other kids had been afraid of Mary because of her shell, yet Mary thought they were shunning her. Fortunately, she now understood and had become friends with many of them. "After you're done, try my grandmother's mixed berry cobbler. She added some vanilla, and that makes it even better than her original recipe."

"Mm." Shelley's appetite instantly spiked at the mere mention of Mrs. Penner's cobblers, which she was known for. "I can't imagine anything better than the original."

"Just wait," Mary said. "It'll knock your socks off." She winked as Shelley laughed. "I thought you'd enjoy that."

Shelley loved how Mary had embraced her life as the wife of a Mennonite farmer without losing all of herself. It must have been difficult knowing what to keep and what to let go. After all, the first fourteen years of Mary's life had been in the lowest trenches of the secular world—not knowing who her father was and with a mother who did who-knows-what to support her. Although Mary rarely mentioned anything about her life before she joined her grandparents in

Pinecraft, she had shared some of the grief over her mother's death at such a difficult age.

After the older women at the table rose to bring out the desserts, Mary leaned toward Shelley. "Jeremiah can't take his eyes off you."

"How would you know?" Shelley asked.

"Because every time I look up, he's staring in this direction, and I'm certain he wouldn't be looking at an old married woman."

"I'm older than you," Shelley countered to cover her embarrassment.

"In years only. Once you get married, you get a leg up on aging." Mary let out a contented sigh. "And I wouldn't trade it for anything in the world. I sure hope you are able to experience the joy of being married to a wonderful husband."

"I thought I would with Peter," Shelley said, instantly regretting mentioning his name. "Sorry."

"Peter made a huge mistake, and I'm pretty sure he knows it now," Mary said. "Clara recently told him she wasn't sure she wanted to stay in Florida because she misses Pennsylvania. When Peter refused to follow her up north, Clara broke off the engagement."

Shelley leaned away from Mary and regarded her with interest. "How do you know all this?" Peter and Clara had started attending a different Mennonite church on the other side of Pinecraft, where Clara's parents attended when they were in town.

"Peter got a job at the lumber store, and Abe talks to him on occasion."

"Good for Peter. I knew he wanted to work there."

"So," Mary began as she folded her arms, "would you want to take Peter back if he was interested?"

"Do you know something?"

A conspiratorial smile formed on Mary's lips. "Maybe."

Shelley slowly shook her head. "After what Peter did to me, I'm not sure if I could ever trust him again."

"Why? The two of you weren't engaged, and from what he told Abe, he didn't realize you expected anything from him."

"Abe didn't tell him—"

"No," Mary said, interrupting her. "But some other people from the church did. He told Abe that he regretted many things, one of them being not noticing how you felt."

"It doesn't really matter now. A lot of time has passed."

"And you're no longer interested in Peter, are you?"

"I have no desire to resume any sort of relationship with Peter...well, except maybe friendship."

"Friendship doesn't preclude a more...romantic relationship," Mary said. "Unless, of course, you have your sights on someone else." She tilted her head toward Jeremiah. "And that someone else is heading this way."

Shelley instinctively turned in the direction of Mary's nod. She met Jeremiah's gaze as he walked toward them with determination.

Mary placed her hand on Shelley's arm. "I need to go see if Grandma needs help."

Jeremiah reached Shelley's side right when Mary left. "I hope I didn't run her off."

"No," Shelley said. "She wanted to go help her grandmother. I think I should probably do a little cleaning."

"I'll help," Jeremiah said without a moment's hesitation. "Maybe we can visit the Ringling Museum of Art afterward." To Shelley's surprise, her mother didn't argue when Shelley asked if it was okay to go to the museum with Jeremiah. All she'd said was, "Be home before dark."

Jeremiah had obviously been there many times because he knew his way around. He pointed out some exhibits and joked around, making her laugh and forget about anything else. When he took her hand on the bus ride back to Pinecraft, Shelley could almost imagine their relationship being normal.

The next morning Jeremiah hopped out of bed with more of a spring in his step than usual. Working beside Shelley yesterday had given him purpose and the feeling that there might be hope for a deeper relationship. To his surprise and delight, her mother hadn't voiced a single objection. He and Shelley had had a real date that had been over way too soon to his liking.

David, the driver he'd arranged through Abe, picked him up at the same time he did every day. "It's good to see you so chipper this early on a Monday morning," David said. "Did you have a good weekend?"

Jeremiah's grin widened. "I sure did." He told David

about the potluck after church, the museum date, and how he felt that he'd made some headway with Shelley. "But I need to take this very slowly because her mom still can't stand me."

"I'm obviously speaking as a complete outsider, but it's been my observation since getting to know many people in your church that most are very forgiving if they know you're sincere."

"Yes, I'm sure that's true most of the time with Mrs. Burkholder, but I'm not so sure when it comes to her daughter. She's very protective of her family."

David told Jeremiah about the courtship with his own wife years ago. "Her dad hated my guts at first, but after we gave him a grandchild, things gradually changed. I think he appreciates me now, but it took years."

Jeremiah paid David and thanked him for the ride before setting up a time to be picked up. "There's nothing to do on my own land today, so I thought I'd swing by Shelley's house after she gets off work."

David waved before taking off. Abe joined Jeremiah on the lawn to give instructions for the day. Jeremiah was glad to have something to do to stay busy and yet have the freedom to think about what he'd say to Shelley.

At two o'clock, Abe walked up to Jeremiah. "Why don't you leave early today? Mary said she thought you might want to walk Shelley home from work."

"Thanks, Abe. I'd better call for a ride now then."

"No need. I called David about fifteen minutes ago, so he should be here any minute."

David arrived five minutes later. "Ready to go see your girl?"

"Let's hope that's how it all turns out. The more I'm with her the more I realize she's the woman I want to be with."

All the way into town, Jeremiah shared his thoughts and feelings about Shelley. "She's one of the most intelligent girls I've ever met, and she has heart. Her younger brother, William, has Down syndrome, and she's very good to him. I understand that she will be responsible for him after their parents can no longer take care of him."

"How do you feel about that?" David asked.

"I'm cool with it. William's a good kid, and he doesn't mind helping out with stuff. I think he likes me, too."

"So all you need to deal with is Shelley's parents?"

"Seems that way," Jeremiah replied as they pulled up in front of the restaurant. "Thanks for the ride." He pulled some bills out of his pocket and handed them to David.

Jeremiah straightened his shirt collar, squared his shoulders, took a deep, cleansing breath, and strode into the restaurant. He glanced around looking for Shelley and spotted her standing by the back corner booth, deep in conversation with someone. She glanced up at him but didn't acknowledge his presence, so he walked toward her. When he got close enough, the person in the booth turned around and looked at him. It was Peter, the guy Shelley had once thought she was in love with.

Chapter Ten

"Hi, Peter." Jeremiah lifted his chin, hoping his trepidation didn't show.

"Jeremiah," Peter said as he stood. "I was just having a nice chat with Shelley, hoping she'd go out with me after work. Would you like to join me for a cup of coffee while I wait for her to finish her shift?"

Jeremiah felt as though he'd hit a wall head-on at full speed. He glanced at Shelley, who didn't look him in the eye. Her discomfort was obvious.

"Uh… I was…uh, on my way home from work, and I wanted to…uh…" What was wrong with him? He cleared his throat. "I really need to get home."

Shelley lifted her gaze and looked at him with an expression he didn't recognize. She wasn't happy about something, but he wasn't sure if he'd caused it, so far be it for him to stick around and risk being a nuisance.

"I guess I'd better go now." He lifted his hand in a half wave and let it fall back down by his side. "See ya."

"Bye, Jeremiah," Peter said as he sat back down.

"It's good you're back. I'm sure you'll be much happier now that you've come to your senses."

A year ago Jeremiah would have fought for the woman he loved. He had to use every ounce of self-restraint to keep his temper under control. Jeremiah wanted to know why Peter was suddenly coming around again, but he was too stunned to see him now to ask. He needed to regroup and figure out what to do next.

Jeremiah walked outside into the bright sunshine, which reminded him the day was still in full swing. He glanced to the left and then to the right as he decided where to go. He didn't want to go home just yet. His father was still at work, and his mother had her quilting group over on Mondays.

He started walking in the opposite direction from home. It was already hot out, even though summer was still weeks away. He could go to the beach, but he didn't feel like facing the curiosity seekers, so he decided against that. For the first time since his car had stalled, he wished he'd bought a replacement.

After several blocks, he found himself at a bus stop. Maybe a ride on the bus would do him some good and at least kill some time.

The bus arrived about five minutes later. Jeremiah boarded the bus and rode for a while, hanging his head, thinking about his options. Seeing Peter with Shelley and knowing their history made his stomach ache. It simply wasn't right. Jeremiah knew for a fact that Peter was no good for Shelley, and he had no right to come back into her life as though he'd done nothing wrong. Jeremiah wasn't perfect, and his past had been checkered with things he regretted, but he'd never hurt Shelley as Peter had.

The biggest problem was how to show Shelley he was better for her than Peter. Until now, he'd felt that he was making some headway with her. The look on her face when their eyes had met flickered in his mind. She didn't seem happy—maybe she was even a touch annoyed—with him stopping by the restaurant. Perhaps he'd deluded himself into thinking she had even a sliver of interest in him.

Jeremiah glanced out the window and spotted a used-car dealership. Maybe he'd check out the lot and see if there was anything he'd feel good about driving. He let the bus driver know he wanted off at the next stop.

As soon as he reached the car lot, the salesman approached. "What can I help you with today, sir? We have some great automobiles in stock just waiting for the right person to drive one of them home."

Jeremiah scanned the rows of cars in all sizes, shapes, and colors. He pointed. "How about that gray one at the end?"

The salesman frowned as he glanced at Jeremiah's watch, the only thing he kept from his time away from the Mennonite church. "I don't know about that one. It's a little weathered and beat up—okay for a kid but not for someone who likes to ride in style. How about this fire-engine red sporty number right over here?"

Jeremiah didn't even look in the direction the salesman pointed. He knew he'd be weak if the right words were said. "No, I want to test-drive the gray car."

With a snort, the salesman backed toward the tiny sales office. "If you insist. I'll go grab the key so you can take it for a spin."

The second the salesman went into the office, Jeremiah allowed himself a brief glimpse of the sports car. His throat tightened, and his skin tingled at the thought of being behind the wheel of that gorgeous piece of machinery. Without hesitation he approached the red car and gently stroked the hood. He could imagine himself cruising the streets of Sarasota, looking all… He stopped, shuddered, and took a step back.

"Hey, I see you've come to your senses," the salesman shouted. "Let me go back inside and get the key so you can drive the car of your dreams. And you won't believe your luck today. We have a special—"

"No, thanks," Jeremiah hollered right back. "I've changed my mind. I don't need to drive any car right now."

"Are you sure?"

Jeremiah didn't bother answering the overly exuberant man, desperate to sell him a car. Instead, he strode as quickly as he could for nearly a quarter of a mile before his resolve crumbled.

That red car sure would be fun to drive, and nothing said he had to buy it. He mentally pictured himself gripping the steering wheel, pulling out onto the highway, testing the engine by pressing his foot harder on the accelerator. After living seventeen years without a car, he'd thoroughly enjoyed the freedom with one. Letting go of his bright orange sports car had been difficult, but he'd had a mixed mission—to reunite with his church and to fulfill his longtime dream of making Shelley his wife. Now, with Peter in the picture beside Shelley, the other half of his mission seemed less attractive.

He did an about-face and walked straight back to the dealership. The little guy who was wiping the windows of a car on the edge of the lot glanced up and did a double take before grinning. "You're back. Does this mean—"

"I'd like the keys to the red sports car," Jeremiah said. "And do you have financing?"

"Yes, of course we have financing. We take care of all your car-buying needs."

Jeremiah watched the man practically skip to his office. He grinned. It didn't take much to make some people happy. He wished he could be one of them.

"I'm sorry, Peter, but I need to go straight home after work," Shelley said.

"How about tomorrow?" His voice sounded urgent. "Maybe we can take a picnic dinner to the beach and—"

"No, not tomorrow either."

"So are you saying you're not interested in me anymore?" Peter tilted his head and stared at her. She wished he wouldn't be so persistent. Although her feelings for him had faded shortly after he'd announced his engagement to Clara, she disliked being put on the spot in such an uncomfortable way, and she didn't feel that she owed him an explanation.

"Peter, I don't need to explain anything to you."

"But we had something special."

She had to take a couple of deep breaths to keep her anger in check. "So special you could get engaged to someone else, leaving me wondering what I did wrong?"

"Nothing, Shelley." He held her gaze for an uncomfortable moment. "You did nothing wrong. I want you back in my life."

She narrowed her eyes. "Where is Clara?"

His jaw tightened for a split second, and then he forced a smile. "She moved back to Pennsylvania. I—I chose not to go with her."

His confession solidified her opinion of him. "It is too late for us. I don't want to be with someone I can't trust."

"I am so sorry, Shelley. After I realized you and William were a package deal, I wasn't sure we were meant to be together." He looked down at the floor and then back up at her with sadness.

Shelley lifted her eyebrows in shock. "Are you saying you lost interest in me because of William? My little brother?"

He nodded with a look of contrition. "I know I was wrong. William is okay. It's just that—"

"You absolutely were wrong." Shelley knew for certain that there was no way she'd ever want to be with Peter now. William was a wonderful human being who would never do anything to hurt anyone. "My brother is the sweetest person I know, and he makes you look like—"

Peter's attention suddenly shifted to something behind her. She spun around and saw Jeremiah behind the wheel of a bright-red sports car as he pulled to a stop in front of the restaurant.

"I thought he decided he didn't need a car," Peter said with a smirk. "Is that what he told you?"

Shelley nodded. She'd half expected him to give in to his desire for another automobile, but she didn't think it would be one like he was now driving. It certainly hadn't taken him long to fall back to his old ways.

She turned around and looked at Peter, who continued standing in front of her smiling. "I'll give you some time to think about us, Shelley, and I'll be back later."

"No, Peter. I've done all the thinking I need to do about us."

"Think some more." With that, he didn't waste another second before striding toward the door.

Without turning around she knew that as Peter left, Jeremiah came inside. His footsteps were soft, but she saw his shadow as he approached.

Jeremiah didn't speak right away, so Shelley slowly turned to meet his silent gaze. "Hi, Jeremiah."

He smiled at her, but she couldn't hide her disappointment. His smile quickly faded. "I just wanted to find out what's going on with us."

Shelley's breath caught in her throat, so she took a step away from Jeremiah to place some distance between them. "With us?"

Jeremiah nodded. "Yes. With us." He shuffled his feet and glanced around the restaurant before settling his gaze back on her. "And between you and Peter."

"I'll answer your last question first. There is nothing going on between Peter and me."

He visibly relaxed. "That's not how it looked, but if you say nothing is going on, I believe you."

"Do you really?" she asked.

"I'm trying." He looked down at her with a closed-mouth grin.

"Now for your first question, that's not quite so simple. I'm not even sure I understand the nature of it."

"C'mon, Shelley, you know how I feel about you."

She thought she knew, but after assuming Peter's intentions, she wasn't about to make the same mistake again. "I'm not positive how you feel, Jeremiah."

"I feel…well, I feel like you and I get along really well, and I like being with you." He shoved his hands in his pockets and cleared his throat. "No, I take that back. I love being with you. When I'm with you, I feel like I can do anything."

Shelley had to try hard not to smile. She'd been hoping Jeremiah felt this way, but there was still the one issue of her parents not approving. She suspected if she could get her mother to come around, her father might follow.

"Well?" he asked. "Aren't you going to say something?"

She lifted her hands to her sides. "I'm not sure what to say, Jeremiah. But honestly, this probably isn't the best place to discuss it."

"What time are you getting off today?"

"Soon. I'm waiting for Mrs. Penner to arrive."

"I'll wait." He sank down in the chair directly behind him.

"But first," she said slowly, "where did you get that car? Is it yours?"

He looked at her and then cast his gaze downward. "No…well, at least not yet. I'm thinking about getting a new set of wheels, and that car just happened to be sitting in the car lot, and I—"

At least he hadn't yet bought the car. Relief flooded Shelley before she considered the fact that she didn't have the right to approve or disapprove of what automobile Jeremiah drove. Or if he even drove one at all.

"What do you think?" he asked softly.

"Does it matter what I think?"

"Yes, of course it does."

Shelley folded her arms and shook her head. "I didn't think you'd be able to resist buying a car, but I have to admit I'm disappointed in the one you chose."

"Too flashy, huh?" His expression was contrite and rather impish.

"*Ya*. It's very flashy. But who am I to cast judgment?"

"I value your opinion, Shelley. If you think the red car is wrong for me, I won't buy it. It's really not that important."

"Then why are you driving it?" She paused before adding, "How important is any car? I thought you were doing just fine without one."

"I guess I have been. It's just that…" He lifted his hands and let them slap his thighs. "I don't know. I came in here and saw you and Peter, and it was frustrating." He hung his head and looked back at her with soulful eyes. "I just reacted."

"That is a concern, Jeremiah. Reactions from bad emotions often involve bad decisions. What happens when something really awful happens? What will your reaction be then?"

Jeremiah grew pensive and rubbed his chin. "That's a good point, Shelley. I suppose I've been reacting all my life."

Shelley knew that. Jeremiah had a tremendous number of good qualities, but the one bad thing about him negated much of the positive. "You need to practice self-restraint."

"I'm working on it."

"I'm sure it takes time."

Jeremiah didn't respond to her last comment. Instead, he gestured toward the door. "Okay, so I probably won't buy the car, but would you like to go for a ride in it before I bring it back?"

She glanced outside at the shiny red car that held no appeal for her. "No, I'd better not."

Jeremiah sensed that he'd taken a step back in his quest to pursue Shelley, simply by showing up in a sports car. He wanted to kick himself a thousand times for not thinking through his decision to stop by during his test-drive. He knew he needed to do something to salvage even a shred of hope to see her again.

"I'm returning the car now, and I'll take the bus home." He took a couple of steps toward the door, stopped, and turned back to face Shelley. "I'm fine without my own wheels. It's just fun sometimes to drive a car like that." Why did he have to keep talking? That last statement eliminated anything he'd done to improve his situation. "But it means absolutely nothing to me."

Shelley grinned at him as though she understood. "I'm sure that's not the case, or you wouldn't be so excited about driving it."

He figured he'd better quit before he dug any deeper. "I'm still returning it. Can we talk soon?"

"Yes, that would be good." Shelley took a step back. "Come back tomorrow." She spun around and was barely past the kitchen door when the bell on the door jingled.

"Jeremiah, what are you still doing here?" The sound of Peter's voice grated Shelley.

"I was just leaving," Jeremiah replied.

Shelley hovered behind the kitchen door, trying to decide what to do. Mr. Penner approached and startled her.

"What is going on, Shelley?" he asked. "You look pale."

"N—nothing. I was just checking to see if Mrs. Penner was here yet."

"She should be here any minute. If you need to leave now—"

"Neh!" Shelley swallowed hard after her sudden outburst. "Sorry, but I can wait for her to arrive."

He pursed his lips and narrowed his eyes as he regarded her. "Is there something I need to know about?" He leaned past her, opened the door to the dining room a couple of inches, and peeked. "Oh, I see the problem. You don't want to leave with Peter, is that right?"

Shelley nodded. "I know I shouldn't worry you with my personal concerns, but I had no idea he was coming back."

"What happened to Clara?"

She explained what she knew. Mr. Penner made a face. "Sounds to me like he wants everything his way."

"I don't know the details about what happened between him and Clara, but I do know that I am no longer interested in him."

"Then tell him you want to go home alone. I've found that it's always best to be direct."

"I already told him that, but it doesn't seem to matter," Shelley replied.

"Would you like for me to talk to him?"

"*Neh*, I don't think that would be a good idea."

Mrs. Penner arrived from the back. "It doesn't look terribly busy today," she said. "Why don't you go on home now, Shelley? I can take over from here."

Shelley glanced back at Mr. Penner, who nodded. "Have one more talk with Peter, and let him know that in no uncertain terms you aren't interested in a relationship with him anymore."

Mrs. Penner planted her fists firmly on her hips and glared first at her husband then at Shelley. "What's the matter with Peter? He'd make some girl a fine husband." She frowned for a moment. "Wait a minute. I thought he was engaged to Clara."

"Why don't you run along, Shelley?" Mr. Penner said. "I'll explain everything to my wife."

Happy to be let off the hook, Shelley removed her apron, grabbed her tote, headed for the back door with only a brief hesitation, and left. She made it nearly a block before she heard Peter's voice behind her.

"Wait up, Shelley. I'll walk you home."

"That won't be necessary, Peter." She quickened her pace, but he caught up with her.

Peter laughed. "You're very independent, as always. I hope Jeremiah doesn't hold on to this silly notion that you would ever be interested in him."

"That's not your concern, Peter."

"Oh, but I think it is. I already told you I made a mistake, and I want to make it up to you. I feel terrible that I hurt you."

"People get hurt all the time. I'm over it."

"I stopped by and saw your mother this morning," Peter said.

Shelley stopped and turned to face Peter. "Why did you do that, Peter?"

"Calm down, Shelley. I care about you and your family, and I thought it would be the right thing to do."

"The right thing to do is leave me alone. You made your feelings for me and my family very clear when you became engaged to Clara. Now let things be."

Peter looked down at the sidewalk and then lifted his gaze to hers. "I can't, Shelley. I'm not getting any younger, and I need a wife."

"Oh, so that's it." She tried to hold back the sarcasm, but it erupted anyway. "You think it's time to get married, and you figured I'd be an easy catch."

"No, that's not it at all." He placed his hand on her shoulder. "You are the ideal woman for me, Shelley. You're everything I want in a wife, and I plan to marry you."

"You should have felt that way months ago. It's too late now."

"I don't think so. Your mother told me she would welcome me into the family."

Shelley felt fury well in her chest. "You told my mother you wanted to marry me?"

He tilted his head to the side. "Yes, I feel it's important to make my intentions clear from the beginning—especially after what happened before. I don't believe in hiding anything."

"You should have asked me first." She started walking again but not as quickly as before. "Now I think you should turn around and leave me alone."

"I can't do that, Shelley. I promised your mother I would join your family for dinner."

"You what?" The shrieking sound of her own voice startled her, so she steadied herself before continuing. "You have no business doing that, Peter. I do not want to marry you."

"Your mother invited me, and I don't want to disappoint her," he argued. "She seems to approve of me as a suitor."

Peter's underhandedness confirmed what she already knew from the moment he'd announced his engagement to Clara—marrying him would have been a huge mistake. They walked the rest of the way to her house in silence.

Jeremiah had just gotten off the bus after returning the car to the dealership when he spotted Shelley and Peter walking toward her house. Curious, he followed them from a distance until they reached the sidewalk in front of Shelley's house. His heart sank, and once again he had to use every bit of self-restraint not to confront them. He didn't think Shelley was trying to deceive him about not wanting to be with Peter, but maybe she wasn't ready to let him go.

Competition had always brought out the worst in Jeremiah, but he couldn't let Shelley go without at least trying to win her over. He'd have to come up with a plan before acting, though, because he knew from experience that acting on impulse would bring him the opposite result of what he wanted.

Jeremiah took a couple of steps toward home when he heard the commotion behind him. Without another thought, he spun around and spotted Shelley's mother frantically waving her arms, sobbing, and trying to talk to Shelley. Peter hung back while Shelley reached out to comfort her mother. Something bad had obviously happened.

Rather than leave, Jeremiah made the hasty decision to see if there was anything he could do to help. He took off running toward the Burkholder house.

Peter's lip curled as he spotted Jeremiah running toward him. "What are you doing here, Jeremiah?"

Jeremiah ignored Peter and focused his attention on Shelley and her mother. "What is going on?"

Shelley's arm remained around her mother's shoulder as she looked at him. "William has disappeared, and no one has any idea where he could be."

"I'll help look for him," Jeremiah said without hesitation.

"We don't need you to help," Peter said. "I think we have this covered without you."

Mrs. Burkholder's expression changed to one of confusion. "That was out of line, Peter. We need all the help we can get."

"*Y-ya, ya*, of course," Peter said. "It's just that… I don't know if Jeremiah knows enough about William to be of much help. He might even be a hindrance…" The look on his face showed that he was aware he didn't have any idea what he was talking about, and he was floundering.

"Where was he last seen?" Jeremiah asked. "And do you remember what he was wearing?"

Mrs. Burkholder sniffled and wiped her nose with her hankie. "He went on break at work, and he didn't come back when the time was up. He was wearing a purple shirt that someone at work gave him. I remember because I wanted him to wear his white shirt, and we argued about it."

"Thanks. I'll start in the area around where he works," Jeremiah said. "Shelley, would you like to come with me, or do you need to stay with your mother?"

Shelley turned to her mother. "What would you like me to do?"

Again, Peter spoke up. "Don't pull this nonsense, Jeremiah. She's needed at home."

Instead of sticking around for a battle of words with Peter, Jeremiah waved. "That's fine. Instead of wasting time talking, I'm going to go look for William now. Someone needs to let all the neighbors know, so they can be on the lookout."

Mrs. Burkholder lifted her finger. "I got a new cell phone. Let me give you my number."

After Jeremiah added her new number to his phone, he sprinted to the bus stop. He rode across town and got off at the car dealership where he'd seen the red sports car. The salesman grinned at him until he realized who

Jeremiah was, and then he scowled and shook his head. "I need a car right away," Jeremiah said.

"You said you weren't in the market for a car," the salesman reminded him.

"I'm not. I just need to borrow one for a little while."

"Unless you're in the market for a car, I can't let you test-drive one. We're not in the business of loaning cars," he said, his voice harsh.

"This is an emergency," Jeremiah said. As he explained what was happening, he witnessed the man's expression softening.

"How do I know you're telling the truth?" the salesman asked.

"I have no idea, but I don't have time to argue. Will you let me use a car or not?"

The man swallowed hard and then nodded. "Tell you what. If you can give me a description, I'll take another car and search for him, too." He glanced down at his feet. "Business has been slow lately, so I don't have anything better to do."

Jeremiah nodded and described William. As soon as he had the keys to one of the cars on the lot, he took off for William's workplace.

William's supervisor gave him all the information he had and handed Jeremiah a card. "If you find him, please call my cell phone."

Chapter Eleven

Jeremiah drove in circles, starting with the block of William's office building. He gradually widened the circle until he spotted the entrance of a city park. On a hunch, he turned and slowly made his way through the mangroves and toward a small clearing of trees. Someone with a purple shirt sat on a picnic bench, so he turned the car toward the small parking area nearby.

As he approached the clearing, he saw William sitting there with his face in his hands. "William?"

The sound of his name caught William's attention, and he looked up. "What are you doing here, Jeremiah?"

"I came looking for you. What's going on?"

William's chin quivered, and he wiped his eyes with the back of his hand. "I had to get away."

"Did something happen?" Jeremiah joined William at the bench.

"Myra tricked me."

"Myra?" Jeremiah pulled the cell phone out of his

pocket. "Give me a minute to let everyone know you're okay, and then I want to hear all about what Myra did."

Jeremiah called Mrs. Burkholder first. The instant she heard that William was safe, she broke down crying and handed the phone to Shelley.

"Is he hurt?" Shelley asked.

"Not physically. I'll take him home as soon as I can."

After he got off the phone with Shelley, he called William's supervisor. "He seems fine."

"That's a relief. We take our job here very seriously, and we don't like to lose our workers."

Next on the list of calls was the salesman from the car dealership. "I found him," Jeremiah said. "As soon as I take him home, I'll return the car."

"Why don't you keep the car for the rest of the day? You might change your mind and decide to buy it." He cleared his throat. "Even if you don't want to buy it, maybe it'll come in handy."

"Thanks," Jeremiah said. "I'll bring it back before you leave."

"I'll be here until seven or eight."

Jeremiah punched the Off button and turned his full attention to William. "Okay, so tell me what happened with Myra."

William grasped the front of his shirt. "Myra gave this to me yesterday and said she thought I would look better in purple instead of my ugly white shirt Mother always wants me to wear." He sniffled. "She says I have funny-looking clothes, and that is why she didn't want to marry me."

Jeremiah understood what William was going through after experiencing it most of his life. "Why did that make you run…er, leave work?"

"When she saw me wearing this shirt, she said I was still funny-looking."

"That was a very mean thing for her to say," Jeremiah said.

"I know. I wanted to take off my shirt and throw it at her, but I didn't have anything else to wear, so I kept my shirt on and left."

"Sometimes people say mean things to me, too."

"Does that make you cry?" William asked.

Jeremiah leaned over and propped his elbows on his thighs as he pondered how to answer the question without being condescending. "It used to, but as I get older and hopefully wiser, I realize when people do that, they're crying out for help."

"What are you talking about?"

"It means that when people say mean things, they aren't talking about you. It's more how they feel about themselves. Happy people who have a good understanding of everyone's differences generally don't try to make other people feel bad."

William's forehead crinkled, and the corners of his mouth tightened. Finally, he nodded. "I believe you."

"When Myra said those mean things, did she make sure other people could hear her?"

"*Ya.* Everyone heard her, and that's what hurts my feelings."

"I don't think she would have said that to you if

no one else were listening. I think she was just trying to show off." Jeremiah straightened up and propped his forearm on William's shoulder. "She was trying to make herself look smart by putting you down."

William turned to face Jeremiah head-on. "Myra has always been a show-off."

"I bet everyone knows that, so they don't think any less of you for what she said."

"Everyone does know," William admitted before growing silent.

"You realize you have a lot of people worried about you, don't you?"

William frowned and nodded. "*Ya*, but I didn't think about that when I left."

Jeremiah stood and gestured for William to follow. "Let's get you back home with your family, and I'll return this car to the dealership."

"Can I ride up front with you?" William asked.

"Yes, of course you can."

William's mood instantly changed as he expressed his excitement over riding in the car. "How fast can you go?"

Jeremiah chuckled. "The speed limit is only forty-five, so that's as fast as we're going."

By the time they arrived at the Burkholder house, William's tears had dried. His mother and sister waited anxiously in the front yard. Peter was nowhere in sight.

Shelley approached the car, flung open the passenger door, and wrapped her arms around William. "We were sick with worry. Don't ever do that to us again."

"Excuse me, Shelley, but I can't get out with you standing in my way."

Shelley laughed and scooted to the side. "Then come on. Mother wants to hug you, too."

After William walked around Shelley toward their mother, Shelley leaned over to talk to Jeremiah. "Thank you for finding my brother. How did you know where to look?"

"I didn't know for sure, but I remembered that he went to a park last time he wandered off, so when I saw the park, I took a chance he might have gone there."

Shelley smiled. "We need to have a long talk with William about not wandering off."

"Or maybe you need to have some way of him letting you know when he needs to get away by himself."

Shelley's smile faded as she shook her head. "He should never be by himself."

"Every man needs to be alone once in a while to think—particularly when he has woman trouble."

"Does this have anything to do with Myra?" Shelley asked.

"I'll let William tell you. But don't force him just yet. He and I talked, and I think he still needs to sort out a few things first."

Shelley's eyes narrowed as her voice deepened. "The only thing he needs to sort out is not scaring our mother half to death."

"Shelley…," Jeremiah began, but he couldn't bring himself to tell her to back off. If something like this had happened to his own family, there was no telling what he'd do.

"Thank you for bringing him home to us. We can take it from here." Shelley held his gaze for a few seconds before joining her mother and brother.

Jeremiah sat and watched the Burkholder family huddle before he pulled away from the curb. All the way to the car dealership, he thought about how little he was trusted—even when he did everything in his power to make things right again.

Lord, I don't know how to make Shelley and her family see that I'm sincere. I've done everything I can think of. If there is anything else I can do, please show me...and make it obvious because I'm blind to subtle messages.

He alternated between praying and talking to himself. Ever since he'd left the church, his life had seemed very shaky. He never doubted that coming back was the right thing to do, but having to constantly prove himself was getting tiresome.

"Someone needs to let Peter know that we've found William," Shelley's mother said after William went to his room. "Shelley, why don't you call him?"

Shelley didn't want to talk to Peter, but she did it anyway so he wouldn't continue looking. When he answered the phone, she could hear the background noise.

"Are you at Penner's?" she asked.

"Um...yes," Peter replied. "William isn't here."

"I know that. He's here with us."

"Oh, good." She didn't hear an ounce of conviction in his voice. "I thought he'd probably find his way home."

"He didn't come back by himself."

"Hey, Shelley, I gotta run. Mrs. Penner just put my plate in front of me, and I don't want my food to get cold."

She clicked off the phone without another word as annoyance coursed through her. Peter didn't care anything about William, or he would have been out there looking for him. Her mother needed to know.

"Did you get ahold of Peter?" Mother asked.

"Yes." Shelley tried to loosen the muscle in her jaw before continuing. "He was at Penner's getting something to eat."

"Poor Peter. He must have worked up an appetite looking for our William."

That was the final straw. "No, Mother, Peter wasn't the least bit worried about William. All Peter thinks about is what Peter wants."

"Shelley! I will not have you talk about Peter like that. He's a fine young man who lost his mind temporarily but finally came to his senses about you."

"That's not true," Shelley said, working hard to keep her voice calm. "He wanted to marry Clara, but she wanted to go back to Pennsylvania, and he wasn't willing to follow her."

"That's because—"

Shelley interrupted her mother. "That's because Peter couldn't have everything he wanted, so he gave her an ultimatum—either Pennsylvania or him. And Clara had the sense to choose Pennsylvania."

"And how would you know this?"

"Peter told me. Mother, I once thought I loved Peter, but now that I look back on our relationship, I realize it was all about him. As long as I made him happy and he got his way, he came around. Clara came along and showed him a little interest, and he turned his back on me like I meant nothing to him."

Mother studied Shelley as though she understood, but that didn't last long. "Like I said, he's come to his senses, and he sees what he almost gave up."

"There's another thing I don't think you realize," Shelley continued. "Peter has never wanted to take on the responsibility for William."

"He doesn't have to."

"If he marries me, he will. I love William, and I will never turn my back on my little brother."

"I love you, too, Shelley," William said from the hallway. "I will always be your little brother." He closed the gap between them and pulled Shelley in for a hug.

As Shelley enjoyed William's embrace, she looked over his shoulder at their mother and wondered what all he'd heard. "How long have you been listening to us, William?" she said softly as she stepped back.

"The first thing I heard you say was that you love me." His grin melted her heart. "I love you, and I love Mother, and I love Father." His chest rose and fell with a deep breath before he added, "And I love Jeremiah.

Did you know that he likes to go to the park to think when he has a bad day?"

"Enough of that," Mother said. "William, go back to your room and think about what you did. We will call for you when it's time for supper."

A flash of pain shot across William's face, but he did as he was told. As soon as he was out of the room, Shelley spun around and faced her mother.

"Did you even bother to hear why William took off?" Shelley asked.

"Neh." Mother folded her arms and scrunched her face. "There is no reason to bother with that. He needs to understand that he is never allowed to run off like he did today."

"Maybe if we took the time to listen to him, he wouldn't feel the need to run away like he does."

"There is never any reason for him to run away. William has as good of a life as we can possibly give him. In fact, I think perhaps we give him too much. I'm going to talk to your father about taking him out of that silly work program."

"You can't do that!" Shelley couldn't believe her mother would even suggest such a thing. "He loves working and having his own money."

"If he loves working so much, then he shouldn't have left and scared us half to death."

Shelley could see that they weren't getting any-where, so she decided to use a different tack. She took a cleansing breath then gestured toward the kitchen. "Why don't we put our heads together and try to figure out some way to help him through this problem he's having with that girl who keeps tormenting him?"

"If it's not her, it will be someone else. Instead of wasting all our time on figuring out how to help him deal with this, we should have him come straight home after school."

Shelley knew how much William valued the small paycheck he brought home, so she decided to stop trying to convince her mother and talk to William. "I'll help you start supper, and then I think I'll go have a chat with William."

"Good idea," Mother said. "Perhaps you can talk some sense into that boy. If he keeps this up, he'll drive me to an early grave."

Rather than continue a conversation that obviously was going nowhere, Shelley helped her mother in silence. Once everything was in the oven, she removed her apron and went to William's room.

She stood at the door of his room and watched him for a few seconds as he sat at his desk staring out the window. "William?"

He turned around and met her gaze. "Hi, Shelley. Is supper ready?"

"No, not yet. Mind if I come in?"

"You can come in." He turned back to the window and pointed. "Look at that redbird out there. I think he forgot he was supposed to fly north."

Shelley leaned over and watched the bird pecking at the food on the bird feeder Father had placed in the backyard. "Why should he fly north when he has it made right here in Sarasota?"

"Because that's where his family and friends are," William replied. "If I was a bird, I wouldn't want them to go away without me."

"But you went away without us," Shelley reminded him.

"That's different. I was upset."

"Maybe the bird is upset about something."

William watched the bird until it had its fill and flew away. He looked directly at Shelley. "Do you think Myra will ever like me again?"

"Maybe, but if I were you, I would concentrate on your job and not so much on whether or not Myra likes you."

"I want her to like me."

Shelley reached for his hand and held it between both of hers. "But why?"

He shrugged. "I don't know. I don't want anyone to not like me."

"Do you like your job?"

"Uh-huh. I like doing work and making money. And Mr. O'Reilly is very nice. He tells me I'm a hard worker, but it really isn't hard at all. I just do what he tells me to do, and that always makes him happy."

"You're supposed to enjoy your work, but that doesn't mean you have to put up with mean-spirited people."

"Shelley, is anyone ever mean to you?"

"Sometimes, but I try not to think about them too

much." She thought about the few rude customers she'd had to deal with. "I have to admit that I'm glad when they leave the restaurant."

"Myra works with me, so she won't leave."

"Are there any nice people there?"

"Uh-huh. Alexander is nice. His mother bakes cupcakes, and sometimes he shares with me during break."

Shelley smiled. "That's very sweet. Why don't you ignore Myra and just be friends with Alexander?"

William thought about that and nodded. "That's what I'm going to do. I'll tell Alexander to ignore Myra, too."

"I don't think God would want you to tell Alexander to do anything like that, but I do think He'd want you to concentrate on the things you like about work."

The sound of Father coming in the door caught their attention. Shelley stood. "Why don't we go set the table and help Mother get everything ready for supper?"

"Is it okay if I come out of my room now?" William asked.

"Yes, I'm sure it's fine." She took him by the hand and led him to the kitchen, where Mother and Father were already deep in conversation.

Chapter Twelve

By Friday, the Burkholder family had settled back down. Shelley's only concern was Mother's increasingly gloomy mood. Each time something happened, she handled the crisis as it happened and then gradually retreated into despondency and remained in bed later than usual. Shelley was concerned about leaving her alone.

Shelley went to her mother's bedside. "Do you want me to stay with you or call someone?"

"No," Mother said. "Go on to work. I'll get up in a few minutes to help William get ready for school."

"I've already done that. He's eating breakfast right now."

In the dim early-morning light, Shelley watched her mother stiffen and then turn over on her other side. When Shelley was much younger, Mother's moods had frightened her, but now she expected them.

"I'll see you this afternoon," Shelley said as she pulled the bedroom door closed behind her.

"Is Mother sick again?" William asked when Shelley joined him in the kitchen.

"I'm not sure. Do you think you can finish and get to school without any help?"

William slammed down his fork. "Of course I can. I am not a baby. When will this family ever understand that I am almost a grown-up?"

Shelley lifted her eyebrows and glared at her younger brother. "William!"

He tucked his chin close to his chest and offered a sheepish look. "Sorry. I know God doesn't like me to get mad."

"I made your lunch, and it's in the sack on the counter."

"Thank you, Shelley." He lifted another forkful of eggs to his mouth but stopped. "I promise I won't run away again, even if Myra says mean things."

"Good. Myra is the one with the problem, not you."

William nodded. "Alexander would never be mean."

Shelley paused and then leaned over the table to look William in the eye. "Just remember that anyone can say hurtful things, but that doesn't mean you should react."

He gave her a puzzled look.

"When people say mean things in the future, either ignore them until they stop, or stand up to them and tell them to stop being so mean. Then drop it."

"Okay." A smile tweaked his lips. "Maybe Alexander's mother will make cupcakes, and he'll bring one to share."

"That would be nice. Just in case she didn't, I put an extra cookie in your lunch bag for your break at work."

Shelley left for work with a heavy heart filled with worry about her mother. She wished she knew what to do about her mother's depression, but no matter how hard she tried to cheer her mother up, nothing seemed to work.

The morning crowd slowly trickled in, and business remained steady for a couple of hours. Jocelyn arrived right before they reached their peak. Shortly after ten o'clock, the bell on the door jingled. When Shelley glanced up, she saw her brother Paul.

"Take a break, Shelley," Mr. Penner said. "Go visit with your brother, and I'll bring over some coffee."

"Good morning, Shelley," Paul said. "I took the morning off to see Mother, but she isn't home."

"I think she is home still, but she's having one of her spells." Shelley glanced around to make sure no one else could hear. "I'm worried about her, Paul. Mother is getting worse."

"I sort of suspected that might be the case since I heard about William running away."

"Who told you?"

Paul blew on his coffee and took a sip. "Father called me this morning. Fortunately, I still have some personal days I can take off from work. Is there anything I can do?"

"I don't know," Shelley admitted. "I might have made matters worse yesterday when I talked back to her." As she told him about the words she and Mother had exchanged, he nodded his understanding. "Mother wants me to agree to marry Peter, but that's not what I want."

Paul smiled and took her hand from across the table. "You don't have to marry Peter just because Mother wants you to, but we need to help her get through whatever she's dealing with."

"I wish I knew what to do."

"There's something else going on that Father told me about, and I wanted to hear your side of the story."

Shelley tilted her head and gave him a questioning look. "What's that?"

"Father says you and Jeremiah have been seeing quite a bit of each other."

She felt the heat rise to her cheeks as she looked down at the table. "Mother doesn't like him."

"It's not that she doesn't like him, Shelley. Mother is afraid of losing another child."

"But she hasn't lost a child."

"I know that, and you know that," Paul said. "But as far as Mother is concerned, she lost me when I married Tammy. And you know what happened when William came along. I think she feels she's being punished."

"No one is punishing Mother but herself."

"Yes, I've known that for a long time," Paul said. "You were forced into being a caretaker when you were quite young, and Mother has always used whatever she could as an excuse to retreat."

"I don't want to dwell on what I can't change."

Paul nodded. "So how is everything here at work? I see Mr. Penner hired someone new."

Shelley took advantage of the change of subject and told him how hard of a worker Jocelyn was. "I like her. She's funny and interesting."

After they finished their coffee, Paul stood. "I'm going back to see about Mother. Thanks for filling me in on what's happening. One of the things I need to do is bring the kids around to see their grandmother. Maybe that'll remind her that she has gained more than she's lost."

Paul left before the lunch rush started. Jocelyn worked as hard as ever, in spite of the deeper bruises still evident on her cheek and right arm. She seemed to enjoy the fact that some of her regular customers made a fuss over her.

Business slowed quickly by midafternoon. Mr. Penner approached Shelley. "Why don't you go on home now? You have been through quite a bit over the past several weeks, and I want you to get some rest."

"I can stick around," she argued.

"*Neh.* I have Jocelyn here to help me now."

A stab of jealousy shot through Shelley, but she quickly recovered. "*Ya*, it's nice to have Jocelyn back."

"I missed this place," Jocelyn said from behind her. "Strange as it may sound, you all are starting to feel like family to me."

Shelley spun around to face Jocelyn. "That isn't strange at all."

Tears sprang to Jocelyn's eyes, but she swiped at

them with the back of her sleeve. "You people came to visit me when I was in the hospital. That's more than my own family did. I appreciate it more than you'll ever know."

"We care about you," Mr. Penner said. "Just like we care about Shelley. No go on home, and get some rest."

"Okay." Shelley pulled off her apron and hung it on the rack in the kitchen. "I'll see you in the morning."

All the way home Shelley thought about her day and how Paul had said he planned to stop by to see Mother. She wondered how their visit went.

When she walked inside, her mother called out from the kitchen. "Shelley, is that you?"

"*Ya*, I'll be right there." As she went to her room to put a few things away, she said a prayer that her mother was in a better mood than she had been earlier.

The instant Shelley arrived in the kitchen, she was stunned by what she saw. Rows of cookies were spread out over the countertops, and the kitchen table had tins stacked high.

"Why are you baking so many cookies, Mother?"

"Here, have one of these, and tell me what you think." Mother offered a heaping platter, and Shelley took a sugar cookie. "Paul and Tammy are bringing the children over tomorrow, and we're going to decorate cookies."

Shelley smiled. "That sounds like fun. I have to work in the morning. Do you know when they'll be here?"

"Late morning. I promised to fix them a picnic to

eat in the backyard, and then we'll come inside to decorate the cookies. I'm sure we'll still be at it when you
get home from work. I can't wait to tell William. He
loves his niece and nephew."

Shelley moved a few tins away from the edge of the
table before sitting down. "What else did you and Paul
talk about?" Mother didn't answer right away. She finished positioning cookies on the baking sheet, stuck it
in the oven and then joined Shelley. "I told Paul about
Peter and Jeremiah."

Shelley's insides twisted. "What did you tell him?"

"I explained how Peter broke your heart and you
can't seem to forgive him."

"That's not exactly—"

Mother lifted a hand to shush her. "We talked about
Jeremiah coming back to the church and trying to court
you." She cleared her throat and glanced down before
looking Shelley in the eye. "Paul talked to me about
forgiveness and trusting that the Lord would guide you
in your decision."

Silence fell between them. Shelley wasn't sure
where Mother was going with this, so she remained
quiet, hoping to hear more.

"I have to admit I argued with him about it, saying
that you could learn to love Peter since you obviously
wanted to marry him before he got…engaged to Clara.
Paul asked me why I was so opposed to Jeremiah, now
that he's returned to the church."

Mother looked directly at Shelley as if waiting for
some sort of response.

"I would like to know that, too," Shelley said softly.

"Paul and I talked for quite a while, and he helped me see some things…" Her voice trailed off as she glanced down at the table before raising her gaze back to Shelley. "He asked what Jeremiah could do to win my favor. We all have sins that must be forgiven, so I couldn't give a good answer." Mother reached over, grasped Shelley's hand, and squeezed it. "I am so sorry for acting the way I did with Jeremiah. After having a child who will never be able to live on his own, then losing Paul, I'm afraid I put all my stock in you. Now I know that isn't the right thing to do."

"First of all, Mother, William is a wonderful brother, and he's doing just fine. Second, you didn't lose Paul."

"*Ya*, I know that now."

"And third, I don't think I ever truly loved Peter. He was simply there, giving me attention at a time when I was worried I might be getting too old to find a husband." She self-consciously smiled at her mother. "And I want to get married and have a family."

"*Ya*, I know that. I will have to get to know Jeremiah before I pass judgment on him."

Shelley lifted both hands and widened her smile. "I'm not even saying Jeremiah is the man I want to marry."

"But you're not saying he's not either," her mother teased.

"True. I really do like him, but like you, I had some reservations about him. I don't ever want to leave the church."

"I can't believe I'm saying this, Shelley, but now you're the one who needs to learn forgiveness. Give Jeremiah a chance."

After they finished their talk, Shelley got up from the table. "I think I'll go for a little walk now. This has been a difficult week."

"Go on ahead. If you want to help with supper, I'll wait until you get back to start it."

Shelley had a lot of thinking to do. As she took off down the street, she inhaled the warm air and allowed it to fill her lungs before slowly exhaling. Today had been filled with surprises—first seeing Paul at the restaurant and then walking in on her mother in such a cheerful mood. Her mother's acceptance of Jeremiah was nothing short of a miracle. But then Shelley remembered how Paul was so good at talking to her and showing her all sides of situations. Shelley wished she had that gift.

Her mind was so filled with the twists and turns in her life that she thought she was imagining the sound of someone calling her name. At first she kept walking, but when she heard it again, she stopped and glanced over her shoulder in time to see Jeremiah jogging toward her.

When he reached her, he stopped to catch his breath. "I've been trying to find you for the past fifteen minutes."

Shelley laughed. "That's not all that long. What did you need?"

"Your mother said you were out walking."

The earth seemed to shift beneath her. "When did you talk to my mother?"

"I just left your house. I stopped by to see if you were home from work yet. When your mother invited me inside, I thought you might be there."

"She invited you in?" She wondered what Jeremiah thought about that.

"Yes." He chuckled. "I was surprised, but the real bombshell was when she asked me to come over tomorrow to help decorate cookies. Any idea what's going on?"

Shelley shook her head. "My brother stopped by and had a talk with her. Apparently, he said something that completely turned her around."

"I think she's just happy Paul is going to bring his family to the Mennonite church."

"*Ya*, that would make her happy. Mother has always dreamed of our whole family attending the same church together."

They resumed walking, at first without talking, until Shelley got up the nerve to ask what was on her mind. "So are you planning to join us?"

"A million wild horses couldn't keep me away."

"Oh, I bet a million horses could," Shelley said with a giggle.

"I'm pretty strong when I'm determined."

"That's good to know."

When Jeremiah reached for her hand, her tummy fluttered. "What else would you like to know?" he asked.

"How's your farm coming along?"

Jeremiah told her all about the crops he'd planted and how he was looking at lemon and lime tree varieties, trying to decide which ones to plant. "There's a whole lot more to farming than most people realize."

"Do you like it?"

"I like it much more than anything I've ever done. This feels like real life to me, and it doesn't hurt to know I'm actually doing something productive."

"I know what you mean," Shelley said. "Mary loves living on the farm and doing a little bit of gardening for canning."

"Can you see yourself doing that?" Jeremiah asked.

Shelley opened her mouth and then closed it and shrugged. She was afraid if she told Jeremiah that she dreamed of having what Mary had—a doting husband who loved the Lord and a home to take care of—she'd scare him away.

"We'll be starting on my house as soon as I choose some house plans." Jeremiah paused. "Would you like to look at the ones I'm considering?"

"I'd love to."

They arrived at the front of Shelley's house and stopped. Jeremiah dropped Shelley's hand but didn't budge from his spot on the sidewalk. "See you tomorrow?"

"I'm working, but I'll come straight home afterward."

"Your mother told me to come early for lunch, but I think I'll wait for you."

"No," Shelley said. "I'd like for you to come early and spend some time with my family."

Jeremiah smiled and nodded. "Okay, since that's what you want, that's exactly what I'll do."

"I don't always expect you to do what I want, Jeremiah."

He howled with laughter. "Trust me, Shelley, I won't."

After Shelley went inside, Jeremiah went on home. He set the table and ate dinner with his parents and then sent them out for ice cream, so he could clean the kitchen.

"Practicing, son?" his dad asked as he lingered for a moment in the kitchen while Jeremiah's mother got her wrap.

Jeremiah glanced up from the sink. "Practicing?"

"Practicing for those times when your future wife needs a hand in the kitchen?" His father winked before leaving with his mother.

That was exactly what Jeremiah was doing, now that his dad mentioned it. He could imagine himself working side by side with Shelley. Now all he had to do was plant the same image in her mind.

He went to the Glick farm early and let Abe know he was going over to the Burkholders' house to decorate cookies. Abe lifted his eyebrows. "Sounds like you are making some headway there."

"I hope so."

"In that case," Abe said, "leave early to check on

your own farm, and then go back into town to be with Shelley's family."

Jeremiah hummed as he did all his tasks. Working hard with his hands kept him busy yet freed his mind. He called David to arrange for his ride, and then he let Abe know when he was about to leave.

"Enjoy yourself," Abe said. "And tell Shelley hi from Mary and me."

Shelley left the restaurant immediately after the lunch crowd dwindled. She practically ran home. Her hands were a little bit unsteady as she opened the front door. If Jeremiah was able to get off early, she knew she'd see him soon.

Mother was in the kitchen arranging all the cookies on the counter. She pointed to the children, who were enjoying a picnic lunch on an old tablecloth. "I was hoping Jeremiah would be here to have lunch with you."

"He said he was going to try to take off early," Shelley said. "Mother, I've been thinking about your change of heart. It happened so fast—I'm confused."

Her mother put down what she was doing, wiped her hands on the towel, and faced Shelley. "Paul found me in my bedroom. At first he didn't know what to say, but when I refused to get up, he got firm with me. He said I was trying too hard to make everything go my way."

Shelley pulled back. "Paul actually said that to you?"

"Ya." Mother hung her head. "In case you're wondering, *ya*, it did make me mad. So mad I hopped up out of bed and gave him a piece of my mind. Once I

was up, he took hold of me and led me to the living room, where he sat me down and said we needed to talk about a lot of things."

Paul sure did have a lot of nerve, and Shelley was grateful. "And all he had to do was mention that Jeremiah deserved a second chance?"

"Oh, it was much more than that, but I will spare you the details. I will say that he used scripture to remind me that the Lord wouldn't want me to hold grudges, now that Jeremiah is claiming to be sorry for what he did."

"How do you feel about Jeremiah?" Shelley asked.

Mother folded her arms and gave Shelley a stern look. "Are you asking me how I'd feel about Jeremiah courting you?"

"Well...*ya*, I s'pose that is what I'm asking."

Her mother's expression turned pleasant, and she actually smiled. "I think I would be okay with that as long as you are sure he is sincere."

Shelley relaxed. "*Ya*, that is important."

A knocking sound at the door got their attention. "I suspect that's Jeremiah. Why don't you get the door while I call the children in to start decorating the cookies I baked? Ask Jeremiah if he's had lunch yet. If not, I'll send the two of you out to the backyard for your own private picnic."

Three weeks later during the church picnic, Jeremiah approached Shelley as she stood with her mother.

"If you don't mind, Mrs. Burkholder, I'd like to have a chat with your daughter."

The twinkle in her mother's eye let Shelley know her mother was in on something she was about to find out. "Of course I don't mind."

"I promised to help put out the desserts," Shelley said. "Can it wait?"

Both Jeremiah and her mother shouted, "No!" in unison.

"Okay then. Let's go." She turned and tucked her hand into the crook of Jeremiah's arm. "Where are we going?"

He gestured toward a waiting car. "I called David to drive us to the beach."

All the way to the beach, David kept glancing at them in his rearview mirror. Even he seemed to know a secret. "How about I drop you off here?" he asked.

"Perfect," Jeremiah said. "Pick us up in about an hour unless I call you to come earlier."

"When are you going to let me in on your secret, Jeremiah?" Shelley asked as she removed her shoes before stepping onto the sand. Then it dawned on her. She turned toward him, smiling. "You've started working on the house!"

"Well," Jeremiah said as he rubbed his neck, "not exactly, but that will be happening soon."

"Then what's so important we had to come all the way here for you to tell me?"

Jeremiah tugged her over toward a private area beside a cluster of palm trees. He opened the towel he'd brought and placed it on the sand. "Have a seat, Shelley."

Once they were seated facing the water, Jeremiah took her hand and kissed the back of it. Neither of them spoke for a few minutes.

Finally, Jeremiah took a deep breath and turned to Shelley. "I've never done this before, so I might be a little bit awkward."

She laughed nervously. "You've never seemed awkward to me, Jeremiah."

"How do I seem to you?"

"You are a very sweet, hardworking man who has asked for forgiveness…and a man who loves the Lord."

"Yes, that is true, but that's not all. I love you, too, Shelley."

A lump formed in her throat, but she managed to reply, "And I love you."

"Good. That makes what I have to say much easier. I would like for you to be my wife."

Shelley remained sitting there, stunned, for a few minutes before she turned to face him. "You've already talked to my parents about this, haven't you?"

"Yes, and William and Paul."

"What did they say?" she asked.

"William jumped up and clapped his hands. Paul said he would be happy to have me for a brother-in-law, and your father shook my hand."

"How about my mother?" Shelley asked.

"She's the only one I was worried about, but she said that if marrying me would make you happy, she'll be happy for us." He looked into her eyes. "Well, what's your answer?"

Shelley flung her arms around Jeremiah's neck and hugged him tight. "Marrying you will make me the happiest woman in Sarasota." She stopped, thought for a moment, and corrected herself. "Make that the happiest woman in the world."

* * * * *

"Isaac, we have a visitor. This is Leah Porte. She's an *Englischer* friend of ours, staying with us a few months. Leah, this is Isaac Sommer."

For a moment Isaac was struck dumb by the newcomer. With her dark hair tamed back under a *kapp*, and her chocolate eyes, he barely noticed the ugly red scar bisecting her right cheek.

Leah stepped forward. "How do you do?"

"Fine, *danke*. Where do you come from?"

"California."

"Please, sit. Both of you." Edith Byler gestured toward the table.

Isaac found himself opposite Leah and gazed at her as the family gathered around the table. When all heads bowed in silence, he found himself praying he could get to know the visitor better.

At once, chatter broke out as the family reached for food.

"We hope you'll have a pleasant stay with us." Ivan Byler scooped corn onto his plate .

"I…I'm not familiar with your day-to-day life." The woman toyed with her fork. "I don't want to be seen as a freeloader."

"What is it you did before you came here?" Ivan asked.

"I was a television journalist," she replied. Isaac saw her touch her wounded cheek and glance toward him. "But after my…my car accident, I couldn't do my job anymore."

LIEXP0820

Journalist! What kind of God-sent coincidence was that? He smiled. "Maybe I should have you write some articles for my magazine."

"Magazine?"

Edith explained, "Isaac started a magazine for Plain people. He uses a computer to create it. The bishop gave him permission."

"An Amish man using a computer?"

"Many *Englischers* have misconceptions of how much technology the *Leit* allows," Ivan intervened. "You won't find computers in our homes, or cell phones. But while we try to live not *of* the world, we still live *in* the world, and sometimes technology is needed to keep our businesses running. So, some bishops have decided a little technology is allowed."

"What's the magazine about?" Leah asked.

"Whatever appeals to Plain people. Farming. Businesses. Land management."

"And you want *me* to write for it?" she asked. "I don't know anything about those topics."

"But that's what a journalist does, ain't so? Learn about new topics," Isaac replied. Her opposition made him more determined. "Besides, you're about to get a crash course while you stay here. Maybe you'll learn something."

"I already said I had no intention of being a freeloader."

He nodded. "*Gut.* Then prove it. You can write me an article about what you learn."

"Sure," she snapped. "How hard could it be?"

He grinned. "You'll find out soon enough."

Don't miss
The Amish Newcomer *by Patrice Lewis,*
available September 2020 wherever
Love Inspired books and ebooks are sold.

LoveInspired.com

LIEXP0820

He stuck his head around the corner of the fasteners aisle just in time to see a tall brunette stagger into the revolving seed display. Some of the packets went flying, but she managed to steady the display before the whole thing toppled. He took in what probably had been a very nice silk blouse and tailored trouser suit before she was drenched in the storm raging outside. The heel on one of the ridiculously high heels she was wearing had snapped off, explaining why she was stumbling around.

"Having a bad morning?"

The woman looked up in annoyance, strands of dark, wet hair falling across her face.

"You could say that. I don't suppose you have a shoe repair place in this town?" She looked at the bright red heel in her hand.

Nate shook his head as he approached her. "Nope. But hand it over. I'll see what I can do."

A perfectly shaped brow arched high. "Why? Are you going to cobble them back together with—" she gestured around widely "—maybe some staples or screws?"

"Technically, what you just described is the definition of cobbling, so yeah. I've got some glue that'll do the trick." He met her gaze calmly. "It'd be a lot easier to do if you'd take the shoe off. Unless you also think I'm a blacksmith?"

He was teasing her. Something about this soaking-wet woman still having so much…regal bearing…amused Nate. He wasn't usually a fan of the pearl-clutching country club set who strutted through Gallant Lake on the weekends and referred to his family's hardware store as "adorable." But he couldn't help admiring this woman's ability to hold on to her superiority while looking like she accidentally went to a water park instead of the business meeting she was dressed for. To be honest, he also admired the figure that expensive red suit was clinging to as it dripped water on his floor.

He held out his hand. "I'm Nate Thomas. This is my store."

She let out an irritated sigh. "Brittany Doyle." She slid her long, slender hand into his and gripped with surprising strength. He held it for just a half second longer than necessary before shaking off the odd current of interest she invoked in him.

Don't miss
Changing His Plans *by Jo McNally,*
available September 2020 wherever
Harlequin Special Edition books and ebooks are sold.

Harlequin.com